D0528590

DAVID FECKHAM;
MY BACKSIDE

DAVID FECKHAM;
MY BACKSIDE

Ivor Baddiel
and Jonny Zucker

ORION

First published in Great Britain in 2004 by

Orion
An imprint of the Orion Publishing Group
Orion House, 5 Upper St Martin's Lane, London WC2H 9EA

A CIP catalogue record for this book is available
from the British Library

ISBN 0 752 86760 1

Typeset by Deltatype Ltd, Birkenhead, Merseyside
Printed in Great Britain by
Clays Ltd, St Ives plc

www.orionbooks.co.uk

CONTENTS

INTRODUCTION:

Real Fun

'I must ask her to pick up some bourbons
on the way home.'

I didn't know whether to laugh or cry. Or masturbate. The enormity of everything that had happened seemed to be hitting me, really hard in the face. Me, David Feckham. It didn't seem possible that I was about to play my first game for Fun in the Sun Timeshare Apartments Ltd XI in the West Costa del Sol League Division 6 (South).

'How did I get here?' I pondered.

And then, suddenly, I just knew – by bus, on a plane, then in a rented car. It was obvious. I just hadn't seen it.

I'd arrived in the dressing room eight hours before kick-off. Three o'clock was still a long way off, but I wanted to be ready. Ready to take the next step on my amazing journey.

Breakfast.

Vivian, Chorlton-Cum-Hardy, King Lear and myself had arrived on the Costa three days earlier. It would have been seven days earlier, but a strike by Spanish air traffic controllers had meant spending four days circling Malaga airport. Still, I was a bit miffed that the Fun in the Sun Timeshare Apartments Ltd representative hadn't waited.

At first, everything seemed so different. The fish and chip shops, the pubs, the Indian restaurants, people's accents – geordie, scouse, brummie, cockney – were all strangely familiar yet unnerving at the same time. But then this was a foreign country, Spain I think they called it, and I knew it would take time for us all to get used to things.

Our first port of call was the Hotel Really Lovely View. Even in its unfinished state I could tell it was plush. Of the two habitable rooms offered to us we let the boys have the one with the ceiling and hoped that there wouldn't be a freak storm that night, the like of which the Costa hadn't seen in thirty years. Sadly luck was against us and that, combined with the fact that due to a local by-law Spanish construction workers can only operate between two and six a.m., meant it wasn't the best first night. Nonetheless, I awoke exhilarated and raring to go.

I left Vivian devouring a breakfast of bottled mineral water and headed to the office. In truth work was the last thing on my mind. It was football that I was interested in. I knew that Fun in the Sun Timeshare Apartments Ltd had a team that played in the local league and I was determined to be their best signing ever. It was said that the legendary Raul had a cousin whose Welsh stepsister's neighbour had once enquired about an apartment. If his name was still on the company's books and if I could get him to contact the step-sister and then get her to contact the cousin and then get her to contact Raul, maybe, just maybe, he could arrange for Real Madrid, yes, the real Real Madrid, to send a scout down to one of our games.

Instantly I imagined myself running out at the Bernabeu alongside David Beckham, hand in hand comparing hair-styles and tattoos. In my mind I heard the frenzied commentary from the gantry: 'Feckham to Beckham, Beckham to Feckham, Feckham to Beckham, Feckham scores – goooooooooooooaaaaaaaaaaaaaaaaaaaalllllllllllll.' I knew they only did that last bit in Brazilian commentaries but I allowed myself a little poetic licence in my fantasies. Then, suddenly, reality kicked in. Beckham wouldn't tolerate my presence at Real. Apart from the fact that I'm better than him, he wouldn't want anyone with such a similar sounding name in the team.

But if Real didn't come in for me, someone else surely would. I knew that the Costa was rife with scouts from all over Europe. I'd even seen two at the airport on arrival, which was why I started playing keepy uppy with King Lear's bag. In hindsight it might have been a mistake to do it on the baggage reclaim carousel, but one of them definitely noticed me, otherwise he wouldn't have alerted the police.

The first person I met on entering the office was Doreen, the company secretary. She was a lady of more mature years, not old exactly, more aged and wrinkled like a half-eaten, three-day-old prune, but I instantly knew that nothing got past her. She'd know everything that I needed to know, so it was imperative that I stayed on the right side of her.

'All right, love,' I said. 'David Feckham. I start work today?'

I held out my hand. She eyed me up and down. I danced the fandango. She drank in my being. I performed a perfect triple salko. She looked into my very soul. I juggled two oranges – Spanish, navel – and a banana – Dominican Republic, fairtrade, organic. She glared right through me. Then, finally, she smiled and held out her hand.

'Doreen,' she said. 'Company secretary. Nothing gets past me. I know everything you need to know, so it's imperative you stay on the right side of me.'

We shook.

I was amazed at how right I'd been about her.

'Have you had your medical yet?' she said lighting a More

menthol cigarette and coughing so violently her blouse burst open.

I'd heard about the Fun in the Sun Timeshare Apartments Ltd medicals, primarily because their acceptance letter informed me I'd need to have one. I was sure it would be a formality, but in footballing terms it could be crucial. At this level it would be insane to play carrying any sort of injury, particularly one that might develop into something worse and lead to a longer lay-off. I knew I was fit, but who could tell what they might find if they stuck one of those long things with a light on the end up my arse? I tried not to show how much stress this was causing me, but as the beads of sweat on my forehead turned into a torrent (so much so that Doreen put a small plastic cup under my chin and drank heartily), I knew if I was unlucky my journey could end here.

Walking into the doctor's surgery I looked around nervously for one of those long things with a light on that they stick up your arse. I saw it hanging on a hook behind the desk next to various other surgical implements. It seemed to be staring right at me and saying, 'Paella flamenco que passé huevos pellota naranja.' Of course I didn't know what it meant then, in fact I still don't, but it certainly shook me up.

'Ah, señor Fuckham,' said the doctor. 'I am Doctor Jesus Soy Sauce Di Asciementos, pleased to meet you.'

'Pleased to meet you,' I said. 'And by the way, it's Feckham.'

'Si, si, that's what I said, Fuckham.'

I didn't see, but let it go, I had more important things on my mind, such as how to distract the doc's attention so that I could dispose of the long thing with the light on the end that they stick up your arse.

4

'Now this won't take a minute,' said Jesus.

Shit, I thought. *Only a minute. I need to act and act fast.* I blurted out the first thing I could think of. 'I know you're sleeping with Doreen.'

'Yes,' said Jesus. 'She's my wife, which reminds me, I must ask her to pick up some bourbons on the way home. Would you excuse me for a moment?'

In the precious few seconds I now had I grabbed the long thing with a light on the end that they stick up your arse and threw it as hard as I could out of the window. It landed, not with a thud as I'd expected, but a yelp, splitting one of the local stray cats in two.

After that the medical went like a dream apart from a tricky moment when the doc said, 'Okay, now all I need to do is take the long thing with a light on the end that they stick up your arse and have a look up your arse and you can go.' He searched high and low for it, but eventually had to use his finger and a hurricane lamp, not nearly as accurate, and declared me fit. I had passed the dreaded medical and was ready to meet the rest of the team.

'I'm expecting big things of you, David. Don't let me down.'

It was Tony, the boss. We were having a private tête-à-tête before meeting the other employees. It was hot, sticky, the air was oppressive. I really didn't know why we had to have the meeting in his sauna.

'I run a tight ship,' he continued. 'You give me a hundred per cent and I'll give you a hundred per cent. We're a team of winners, Davy boy. Are you a winner?'

'Just give me the opportunity and I'll prove it to you,' I said. 'I'm itching to get me boots on, stride out on the pitch and bring home the silverware. I can do twenty-three keepy uppies with my foot and four with my head. I can play anywhere, defence, midfield, up front. I've got two good feet, great technique, I'm quick and I've got the experience you need.'

'What the fuck are you talking about?'

'The Fun in the Sun Timeshare Apartments Ltd football team. I'm going to help you win the West Costa del Sol League Divison 6 (South), and after that, who knows, we could go all the way.'

'Look, if you want to play for that bunch of plonkers, speak to Ian. They're so desperate they'll take anyone. What I want from you is sales, sales, sales. We'll start you at 500 euros a month plus commission. Okay?'

But I wasn't listening. I was already out of the door and making a beeline for Ian at the new employees' cheese and wine reception. I just wish I'd remembered my towel.

'And this is Barry, he's our right back, they call him El Burro, the donkey, and it's not because of you know what.'

Ian bellowed with laughter. He was a big man, some would say clinically obese, with a laugh that was not so much infectious as really grating and horrible. He was introducing me to my new team-mates.

'And this here is Sid, he's got two left feet, and that's on a good day.'

Ian introduced me to the other players and laughed at every one of them. I felt a little sick.

I'd met them all now and the spotlight was on me. It was my turn to say something. Fortunately, I'd prepared a speech. Unfortunately, I'd forgotten to bring it. Fortunately, I thought I could remember most of it. Unfortunately, I was wrong.

'Er, ta, thanks Ian, great to meet you all.'

It wasn't exactly what I'd intended to say, but the gist was the same and the lads seemed to like it. Next thing I knew someone had tossed a ball to me. I attempted to trap it, but in the high heels I'd been given to wear after the sauna, I only succeeded in puncturing the ball. The others roared with laughter though and I knew that no matter how serious things got out on the pitch, in the dressing room I was going to be the joker once again.

That was my destiny and it had been waiting for me since the moment I first kicked a football.

CHAPTER 1:

A new Pelé/Maradona/Cruyff/Best is born

'Pass the ketchup David.'

I vividly remember my first ever game of football.

It was on Christmas Day, three weeks before I celebrated my second birthday. The whole house was covered in 'flashing' multicoloured lights that perpetually remained on green. An enormous Christmas tree towered majestically in the front room: Dad had 'borrowed' it the day before from outside the corner shop. Unfortunately for him, the proprietor, Mr Givens, had chained it to some weighty goods to prevent people doing just that. This meant Dad had had to lug it home with eight sacks of Maris Piper potatoes and a box of charcoal briquettes trailing noisily behind him.

I'd only experienced one Feckham Christmas and couldn't really remember it, but I did know that gifts were allocated in our house on a strictly first-come-first-served basis. This process entailed four stages. *Stage One* involved all of the presents being placed under the tree. *Stage Two* referred to the 'stalking' process, whereby everyone was free to monitor how many presents there were and in what order they had been strategically placed. *Stage Three* was all about Dad shouting the word 'Go!' at a moment of his choosing (clearly giving him a massive advantage, as he often did this when no one else was in the house). *Stage Four* followed this command and involved each person grappling for themselves. Whoever held on to a present for more than ten seconds got to keep it.

But Mum was still feeling some discomfort from the slipped disc she'd picked up during this ritual the previous year and insisted on doing it 'properly' this time.

My older sister Katie (aged five) went first. She was more than happy with her Motorway Service Station Barbie complete with overpriced plastic sandwiches and a miserable-looking RAC man. My younger sister Clare (aged six months) received a lamb's teething ring – snapped up by Mum at an end-of-season city farm sale.

I was nearly hysterical when it came to my gift and tore at the paper wildly. When I finally opened it I couldn't believe my eyes – *The Joy of Sex* by Dr Alex Comfort MD.

'Oh, sorry,' said Dad. 'That's from me to your Mum. Here's yours.'

He handed me a cardboard box. I pulled open the flaps. Inside it was a plastic football – the type that if kicked hard enough orbits Mars and comes back two months later. Until then, I'd shown no interest in football whatsoever, and Dad had decided it was time for me to learn the basic rudiments of the 'beautiful game'.

I looked at this shiny white orb with awe and delight, unsure at first what it was. When Dad whispered in my ear, 'It's a football you twat,' I got the message. I ached to ask what I was supposed to do with it, but didn't feel this question would endear me to him.

Dad then opened his gift: a family pack of extra-long matches. He loved matches. He could do all sorts of remarkable tricks with them and some of these didn't involve him burning himself. There had been talk at one stage of him joining the Magic Circle but he couldn't afford a comedy bow tie so he missed his appointment. He did do garden bonfires for everyone in our street though, even when they'd specifically told him not to.

You could see he was chuffed with his gift because he cackled with glee and set fire to Mum's hair.

'Only joking,' he guffawed as he sprayed her with a unit from his vast collection of fire extinguishers. He'd collected these ever since his early twenties and would never leave a public building without one.

As soon as the last helping of Christmas pudding had been guzzled, we cleared the chairs in the front room and Dad gave me a short lecture (with overheads) about the skills needed to make a half-decent footballer. I listened intently, attempting to take notes with the large crayons Nan had given me and holding my new ball tightly to my chest. But being one, all I succeeded in doing was to create a swirling mass of waxy debris on the paper (I've kept those notes to this day and still refer to them from time to time). Then Dad announced it was time for my first match – him versus me.

I'd only been walking for eight months, so it was no surprise that he netted two early goals. But his defending was sloppy and I quickly managed to pull a couple back. The game went on in this fashion – real end to end stuff. The whole family was captivated. I can still remember Mum and my sisters standing on the makeshift terrace they'd fashioned out of a balsawood nativity set, chanting, 'You're going to get your fucking head kicked in.' At 5–5 you could feel the tension crackling in the air. With one minute to go, Dad awarded himself a penalty. I stood in front of my goal – an ageing, foam-sprouting, brown sofa – wobbling my knees to put him off. He struck the ball forcefully and it knocked me over before smashing one of the windows.

Mum was furious.

'You moved before he took the kick!' she shouted at me,

and made him take it again. This time I dived behind the fish tank, seconds before another window was taken out. As I tiptoed my way through the shards of broken glass, I knew that I was hooked.

Football was definitely for me.

Dad was delighted that I now showed an interest in the game and instructed me to dedicate myself to honing my skills. He explained that I'd have to carry out this task by myself, as he was always amazingly busy. Any spare time he did have he liked to spend with his best mate, Harry Taylor, and the local pigeon fanciers' society. I accepted this explanation graciously and told him that I'd practise and practise until one day he'd be proud of me. He winked at me and told me to go and bother someone else. I liked to think of him not as an absent father, but as a father who was never there.

So from the ages of two to four, I spent hours kicking a ball outside against a wall at the back of the house. Unfortunately it wasn't our house and the couple who lived there claimed to their insurance company that the subsidence on their property was down to me. (After fourteen years and £27,000 in legal costs they were finally awarded £85.)

When I turned five, kids started knocking on our front door. Whenever I heard this sound, I'd grab my lightweight football, run down the hall, my heart pulsating with excitement, and fling open the door. My mind spun with the possibilities that could be awaiting me. Would it be a one-on-one kick-around? Maybe there'd be a five-a-side game waiting? Or perhaps it was going to be a full eleven-a-side affair with laminated shirts and man-sized goalposts?

'Can Katie come and play?'

It was always the same question.

Katie would emerge from the kitchen where she'd been putting the fridge back together having taken it apart moments earlier (this skill stood her in good stead because she's now a senior repair operative for a fruit-machine emporium).

Crushed with disappointment I'd ask whoever it was at the door if I could tag along and perhaps add a game of football to their itinerary.

'Sod off, short arse,' was the usual reply.

I looked on forlornly as Katie left the house and ran off with her mates.

'Don't worry,' Mum would say, appearing in the hall behind me, holding Clare, who'd be napping in the cat's basket or eating a length of toaster flex, 'one day that knock will be for you.'

But it never was.

Katie was really good about it. She told me to stop answering the door and butt out of her life. I appreciated her sensitivity and gradually trained myself like a reverse Pavlovian dog to stop dribbling when the knock came.

I began to wonder if my lack of visitors was down to the fact that no one in our locality played football. But I soon found out it was because I had no friends. That was when I realised it was time for me to go out and *find* a game.

Luckily, it wasn't long before I discovered where some of the local kids hung out at weekends, by an enormous pile of junk on the waste ground behind The Roxy cinema – known as 'the Dump'. One Sunday afternoon I found myself down there, drawn by the frenzied shouting and the whiff of decaying timber.

About twenty lads were in the middle of a game I later came to know as 'Bombers'. The rules were simple. Every-one threw great chunks of rusting metal at each other with the winner being the one who inflicted most injuries. Twenty minutes later, Trev, their self-appointed leader, announced he'd won and wound the game up. A couple of lads were hobbling around on makeshift crutches and one boy lay on top of a rusting fridge, moaning: 'Drink milk. It's calcium rich.'

Trev took no notice of them. He'd spied me watching on the sidelines and asked if I wanted to join in with the next game.

'Are you up for it?' he bellowed at me.

I shook my head firmly.

'Good,' he replied, 'you're in.'

The next game was called 'Journey To The Earth's Core', in which you had to see how far into the junk pile you could crawl without dying. The kids down there took it really seriously and some had full bio-hazard knitwear to help them through the ordeal.

It was a hideous and yet gratifying experience and I emerged relatively unscathed at the end of the game. (I'd made it a long way into the pile, but my progress was blocked by a large section of a brick wall.) Trev nodded at me silently as I brushed some iron filings off my jumper. I wasn't sure if this look meant *Well done you've passed your initiation* or *Look at me again and you're dead*.

Either way, I loved this visit and decided that I'd finally come across a crew who were on my wavelength. I started going to the Dump every weekend. Many of the kids were hostile to me at first. They didn't like admitting new members to their gang. But for some reason, Trev accepted me and I never really knew if this was because of my positive attitude or the pound coins I gave him that I'd nicked from Mum's purse.

One Saturday, I suggested that the Dump would be a great place to stage a football match. After hitting me with a piece of wood, Trev announced that he'd just had a brilliant idea. The Dump would be a great place to stage a football match. There were several nods of assent and he began to organise his workers. We used the carcasses of two burnt-out cars as goals and an old tin of chocolate digestives as the ball. Everyone loved playing in the match, except for the kids in bare feet.

Soon these football games at the Dump became a regular weekend fixture. And some of us actually began to get near the ball instead of just chasing it around in a huge pack. By some miracle, Trev was never on the losing side in any of these matches. I reckoned it might have something to do with the endless free kicks he took one centimetre in front of the opposing goal.

One day, a boy called Leon appeared at the Dump waving his arms frantically in the air. We thought he had something important to tell us, but he'd just passed his Air Traffic Controller exams and was in the middle of a shift. We dived to the ground as a Boeing 747 roared over millimetres above us.

After we'd picked ourselves up, Trev started walking menacingly towards Leon. But Leon sensing imminent danger blurted out, 'I've discovered this amazing grass pitch behind an old paper factory. It apparently belongs to a local sports club that only use it for big games. Maybe we could play our football matches there.'

Trev was impressed with the speed and clarity of this statement.

'Let's check it out,' he commanded.

We traipsed after Leon, spreading out in case the police swooped on us as potential urban terrorists. Apart from doing over a couple of houses and spraying several taglines of obscene graffiti on the underside of a few bridges, nothing could have been further from our minds. We had a purpose. We were heading to a destination.

Leon had been right. The pitch did look fantastic. We gaped through the enormous perimeter fence encircling it. It was such an imposing sight. We needed someone to take charge. Trev obliged and whispered something to a tiny kid called Mutt, who sped home on his space hopper and returned ten minutes later with some industrial strength wire cutters.

Trev did the honours and moments later we were pouring through the giant hole in the fence. As we reached the pitch, we felt a sense of communal destiny. This was going to be *our* place. The recently mowed grass was so lush and aromatic that a couple of boys tried smoking it. They were impressed and praised its healing powers but both came out in a nasty elbow rash the following day.

I still had my plastic ball and I kicked it into the air. Sadly, I sliced it and the ball was nearly lost in the canal, but Mutt was a fast little guy and bounded off to retrieve it. Trev looked around with a smirk of satisfaction. He enjoyed the thought of being the top dog in this environment.

Our first match there was a thrilling spectacle. Trev's side won 13–0 and he was overjoyed as he blew the final whistle. There were a few rumblings of discontent from a couple of the other players. They were miffed that Trev had been the only player allowed on the pitch. But the rest of us understood the score. Trev could have his day if it meant that this place could become our second home. Leon was held aloft on our shoulders as the hero who'd led us to this promised land. He basked in the glory and still managed to divert a couple of low-flying aircraft to Stansted.

From that second, we played on this amazing surface almost every day – our games only interrupted by the bad-tempered groundsman, Stan, who nibbled Kit-Kats and shouted obscenities at us from his tiny wooden hut.

Playing there was a truly incredible experience. It became my field of dreams, not only because when I strode across that turf I fantasised about becoming a legendary hero, but also because I sometimes slept there.

On those nights as I lay under the stars in an old sleeping bag, I often had a recurring vision. In it, I had just scored the winning goal in the FA Cup final in front of a capacity crowd. As the ball punched the back of the net, I turned and ran in triumph towards my team's supporters. But as I approached the stand where they were all sitting, they suddenly turned into giraffes and began chasing me across the pitch, braying with anger and hostility. As I sped over the turf I spotted a huge bag of Caesar salad standing in the centre circle with the words 'washed and ready to eat' splashed across it in gold letters. As I leapt inside this bag, the sachet of dressing suddenly sprouted three tentacles and reached out to grab me. I frantically managed to extricate myself and climbed towards the bottom of the bag where a large door led to a tunnel marked 'This way if you want to live.' I was almost through this door, when a sly anchovy blocked my path and said with a Texan drawl: 'What's up, motherfucker?' It was at this point that I always woke up.

I once mentioned this dream to my mum at tea-time.

'Pass the ketchup, David,' she replied.

I passed her the mayonnaise, unsure if she was playing some weird psychological game with me or simply placing greater importance on complementary culinary sauces than on the study of the unconscious.

Although I never told anyone in my family about this remarkable pitch, somehow Dad got to hear about it and turned up one Saturday with a pad and two betting shop pens. He'd just had a big win on the dogs and was in a convivial mood. I felt a knot tie in my stomach and cursed myself for taking part in the rope-eating competition that Trev had organised earlier that day.

Dad had never watched me play in a proper game, and I half-waved at him, not knowing if I should be pleased or concerned to see him there. He was holding up a wad of tenners, displaying his winnings for all to see. I wondered how he'd discovered this sacred place.

I played extra hard in the game, constantly conscious that Dad was on the touchline making notes. When the game was over, I was the last player to leave the pitch and shyly approached him. An unsmoked cigarette dangled from his parched lips as he finished writing something down on the pad and rearranged the grubby ten-pound notes in his wallet.

As I got nearer, I gave him that age-old, son-to-father look. The one that whispers yearningly: *What do you reckon Dad? What's the verdict? How did I play?*

He looked at me fondly, with those warm, shining eyes.

'You were rubbish,' he said.

CHAPTER 2:

A new Pelé/Maradona/Cruyff/Best gets a bit older

'Always kick the ball with your feet son.'

My parents, Reg and Sheila, have always been inspirational figures for me.

On Mum's side I follow a proud lineage of blacksmiths. As her mother, my grandmother, and her grandfather, my great-great-great-grandfather, had done, Mum spent many years plying her trade within rented stables in Walthamstow. She only gave this up when I was twenty, as there were no more horses to shoe in the East 17 postal district and because anvils had become scarce due, ironically, to a strike by the very blacksmiths who made them. Accepting the modern age, she moved to a job in a call centre. There, she was employed to make enquiries about the dimensions of people's pockmarks, on behalf of an acne cream manufacturer. The management were very liberal (they were trying to win the 'Britain's most worker-friendly business' award) and if tiredness overwhelmed any of their staff, they provided them with two duck-and-down pillows and a mini duvet. Their philosophy was that calls made whilst sleeping were equally as valid as those made during waking hours. Mum still works there today.

Dad, on the other hand, was a businessman of the wheeler-dealer variety. In this he was something of a disappointment to his father, my grandfather, and his grandfather, my great-great-great-great-grandfather, both of whom were out-and-out career criminals. Dad's granddad, Neville Feckham, was a gin seller, who was picked up by the 'Peelers' several times for heavily diluting his spirits with gripe water. Dad's dad, Howard Feckham, was involved in the 'Great Chicken Snatch' of 1961 – the one that culminated in the legendary St David's Day scrambled-egg 'cookout' on Wandsworth Common and has since been immortalised in Steven Spielberg's *The Legendary St David's Day Scrambled Egg Cookout*, starring Dame Judi Dench, Scarlett Johansson and Nicholas Parsons.

Both Neville and Howard looked down upon the cheeky-chappie-who-ran-the-gauntlet-of-the-law-but-actually-had-a-heart-of-gold type. They'd hoped Reg might be the first Feckham to go into serious crime: armed robbery, drug-dealing, contract violence, that sort of thing. But it wasn't to be. No matter how many toy post offices they gave him as a kid, he was always more likely to store them in his toy lock-up than burst in with his toy sawn-off shotgun threatening to waste any toy fucker who moved. They even got him a Saturday job with the Krays; he had to check up on people the cuddly East End gangsters had earmarked to be murdered and decide whether they were 'their own', and thus acceptable to be done away with, or 'not their own', and thus untouchable. It hadn't helped though and he left school at fourteen (with 200 pencil sharpeners, which he sold to a local newsagent for ten bob).

The rift between Mum and Dad as to which life path I should follow was intense. Mum was determined I should follow her and become a blacksmith. Dad wanted me to run a warehouse so I could 'supply' him with goods for his lock-up.

Apart from debating key life issues with Mum, the other

thing Dad was passionate about was Manchester United. They were his team and that was the end of it. It didn't matter to him that he'd never seen them play, didn't know who their players were, never looked out for their result on a Saturday, never talked about them in the pub and never watched them on television. They'd been responsible for the greatest moment in his life and in return they got his support. When he was just starting out in the dodgy dealer business he'd bought a job lot of hand towels and flannels emblazoned with the Manchester United crest. He'd expected to make only a small profit, but, unknown to him, on the day he went out selling them United were in town to play West Ham. The whole area was flooded with United supporters desperate for a good wash and rub down before the game. He sold every last towel and flannel, plus all of the poorly designed Latvian showerheads he had in stock. To this day I've never seen him so pissed. From then on Manchester United were the only team for him and it was drummed into all of us that if we wanted his love, parental approval and attention, we'd be wise to follow suit.

Dad was always running around chasing some deal or other. There was even one period of six months when I didn't see him at all. Naturally I assumed he was banged up, but it turned out he'd bought a lorry-load of keys and then lost his own set amongst them. Since there was no way Mum would lend him hers to get another set cut, it had taken him the entire six months to find his again so he could let himself back in. As a father now myself I'm determined not to be like that with Chorlton-Cum-Hardy and King Lear. They're the most important things in my life, after football and beer obviously, and I'll always be there for them.

On my seventh birthday, however, Dad declared that things were going to change. He'd had a lucky break and landed a hundred hi-fi systems that malfunctioned after playing their ninth CD. He flogged them all in a car boot sale in Rotherham and was pretty certain that nobody would trace him back to the East End. The money was good and meant he'd have some time for his son, so he started taking me down to the local park on Sundays.

I'll never forget those afternoons, well some of them I will obviously, but I'm really talking about the overall feeling of them rather than each individual one. They were special because more than anything they cemented my belief that I was going to be a footballer. I was going to make it. The games with the Dump lads had fizzled out after Trev started digging up squares of turf and selling them to local garden centres. And I couldn't get into the school team because I never went to school. So those afternoons with Dad were all I had. His motive was ostensibly to teach me a thing or two, but if there were other dads around (and there always were) he'd join them for a kickabout and use me as a goalpost. One bitterly cold December day after he'd finished playing in one of these games, he left me out in the snow, standing completely straight, for a couple of hours whilst he went into the park café for a cup of milky tea with half a sugar or a cube if they had cubes.

Dad wasn't much of a footballer. He turned out for a couple of local teams and nearly had a trial for a team that wasn't so local, but I think he knew he wasn't going to make the grade. Being a pro isn't just about having the ability. You've got to have the right attitude. And a nickname, ending in 'y'. Dad had neither. He played in defence and was the sort of player who always gave fifty-three per cent. As for a nickname, he was never liked or hated enough to have one. He had no outstanding charac-teristic that could be pinned on him and form the basis of one and physically he wasn't quite deformed enough in any one area. (All together his deformities made him grotesque, but his team-mates never got to see his anal warts, tongue boils or cochlea carbuncles; if they had I feel sure they would have called him something witty and clever like 'warty' or 'boily'). On one occasion he tried to claim 'Daddy' as his nickname, as that's what I called him and it ended in a 'y', but for some reason it didn't stick.

On the whole I enjoyed those park outings with Dad, but I did get slightly frustrated when he hogged the ball for hours at a time, dribbling around me and commenting on his moves in the style of a frenzied local radio reporter. I can still hear him to this day.

'Feckham, playing from left to right as we look, picks up the ball just inside his opponent's half. He takes it past David Feckham, he takes it past him again, and again and again and again. He really is making his opponent look like a complete idiot, in fact I've never seen anyone made to look so utterly stupid.'

What I wanted was tuition. There were certain areas of my game that needed fine-tuning. I wasn't very good at kicking, passing, controlling, heading, shooting, crossing, catching or throwing. Surely, I reasoned to myself, we could work on those aspects of the game.

'Dad,' I'd say after we'd been in the park about three to four hours. 'Can we work on my shooting now?'

'Yeah, son, yeah,' he'd reply. 'In a minute.'

Then we'd carry on as before for another two hours before Dad finally started my instruction. It was worth the wait though. The nuggets of advice Dad passed on to me were invaluable. They were like mantras; I still repeat them to myself today.

'Always kick the ball with your feet, son,' was one he used to say a lot.

Then there was 'Head the ball when it's in the air,' and 'If anyone nutmegs you, be sure to get their name and address.'

I've started passing Dad's tips on to Chorlton-Cum-Hardy, but I think he might be a little too young to appreciate them at the moment. He just laughs when I say them now, but I'm sure in time he'll come to understand them.

It was about this time that Uncle Terry came looking for me. We called him Uncle Terry even though he wasn't our uncle and his name wasn't Terry. Dad knew him from way back and had never really liked him. Mum didn't like him either. She never trusted any man (or woman) with facial hair, and Uncle Terry's thick beard gave her the collywobbles. Thinking about it Katie and Clare weren't much fond of him and neither was I, but there was nothing we could do about it; he was our Uncle Terry and that was that.

On this occasion Uncle Terry stood outside the front door, explaining to Dad the reason for his visit. As usual when Terry called I was cowering in the cupboard under the stairs along with my sisters, and Mum. It was dark, damp and smelt of cauliflower cheese, but I could just about make out their conversation.

'Don't worry, Reg, nothing will happen to David. I'll look after him,' said Terry.

'Sod him,' said Dad. 'It's my ball I'm worried about. It's real leather, cost me three and six [about £270 in today's money].'

'Listen, if this goes well I'll see you right and you'll be able to afford all the balls you want. Now just go get the little c—'

I didn't hear the rest because the cauliflower cheese Mum was cooking bubbled over and scalded Katie. The next thing

I knew Dad was hauling me out of the cupboard for a meeting with Terry.

It transpired that Terry had a heart after all. He said that he knew this old chap whose nephew was a scout for United. Apparently the old fellow ran a really quiet sub post office in a small village outside Southend. Terry reckoned that if me and some mates had a bit of a kickabout outside his post office, he might ring his nephew and put in a good word for me. I was so happy I tried to hug Uncle Terry, but went off the idea when I spotted a maggot in his beard.

The day of the big game was set for the following Wednesday at 10.30 in the morning. Terry said that would be the best time as it was especially quiet then and the old boy would be able to watch me without any disturbances.

In the four days leading up to the game I hardly slept a wink, my mind racing with the possibilities. I guess it must have been the excitement, but it could have been all the coffee I was drinking.

Strangely, though, when the big day came I completely overslept and nearly missed everything. It makes me laugh now to think how differently things might have turned out if Dad hadn't come into my room and thrown a bucket of icy cold water over me. But that was typical of him: always thinking of others before himself.

The mates I'd enrolled for the kickabout were Derek Parker who lived three doors away and Barry Thompson who didn't. I called them Del and Baz for short and DelDelDelDelDel and BazBazBazBazBaz for long. I hadn't told them the real reason for the game, it didn't seem fair to get their hopes up when I knew they wouldn't stand a cat in hell's chance of ever making it in football. I lost touch with Del a while ago, though the last I heard he was working for the government, planting weapons of mass destruction in Iraq. Baz and I are still good mates though.

He's a semi-professional bar billiards player now and makes a decent enough living at it, though he earns nothing like what the top boys get.

I opened the door to Del and Baz, still wet through from the soaking Dad had given me.

'You r-r-r-r-r-ready then l-l-l-l-l-l-l-l-lads,' I said shivering and turning blue.

'Yeah,' they replied.

Then, before I could dry off or change out of my pyjamas Terry turned up in his transit van.

'Right,' he said, his beard releasing the remnants of breakfast as he spoke. 'Get in.'

Next thing I knew we were hurtling towards Southend. Terry seemed almost as excited as I was. He had a maniacal grin on his face and was smoking roll-up cigarette after roll-up cigarette, as I'm sure I would have been if I'd been older and a smoker. It made me realise how much Terry cared about me. Thinking that he was doing all this for me made me feel so close to him. In fact I don't think I've ever felt closer to anyone than at that moment.

Terry parked round the corner from the post office and we all got out of the van. It was time for our pre-match instructions. If I was to perform at the very best of my ability the words Terry was about to say could be crucial; they could determine the path of my whole life.

'Now then, I want you to play right in front of the window, that way the old geezer will be able to see you, right?'

'Why do we want him to see us?' asked Baz.

I'd been expecting this. I'd got Del and Baz there by promising them a pair of Mum's knickers each, if they helped out. Not knowing our real purpose meant they were bound to ask some awkward questions, but I was ready.

'Because,' I started, but before I could finish, Terry had grabbed Baz by the neck and was lifting him off the ground.

'Because I say so, and if you don't do what I say your pathetic little life ain't going to be worth living, got that, runt?'

It wasn't pretty, but then I knew that football was a man's game. Some managers could dish it out and if you couldn't take it you weren't going to make it. I knew Terry was only putting on a bit of a show for my benefit, because he wanted me to be the best.

So, with Dad's leather ball in my hands, we walked round the corner to the post office.

'Right, three and in,' I said as we got to the window. By now I was really buzzing. Every sinew in my body was taut. Of course back then I didn't know what sinew or taut meant, and I still don't really now, but it does describe exactly how I felt.

'Del, you go in goal,' I said.

Del stood in front of the window. There was no way the old guy in the shop was going to miss me. He'd be on to his nephew any second.

I dropped the ball at my feet. I was still quite cold and wearing pyjamas, but in my head I was at Wembley Stadium, kicking off the cup final. I rounded Baz easily enough, he was still sobbing from earlier, and found myself in a one-to-one with Del, the goalie.

As he approached to narrow the angle Dad's words flashed through my mind. Unfortunately, probably due to the excitement and everything, they got muddled up, and what I heard was, 'Always kick the ball with your head, son'. Next thing I knew I was sprawled on the tarmac, trying to nod the ball past Del with my head, scraping my cheek on the gravel in doing so, and opening up a long, deep cut. That, coupled with the fact that Del had opted to kick the ball away and in fact made contact with my head, meant I was pretty dazed. But on the plus side, I had a penalty. (Well, he'd kicked me in the head.)

Of course Del was sent off for the foul and that meant Baz, whose whole body was, by this time, quivering with uncontrollable sobs, had to go in goal.

I lined up the kick. The sort of classy player I was, I knew Baz would be expecting me to place it. So, to fool him, I blasted it. It hit him full on in the face, knocking him backwards and through the window. That got us noticed right enough. The old boy came charging out of the door shouting and screaming blue murder.

Me and Del legged it and hid round a corner. From where we were we could just about see the old guy's walking stick as it came smashing down on Baz's skull. We thought about going back to help him and were just about to when an amazing thing happened. A bloke wearing a pair of tights over his face and carrying a baseball bat ran into the post office. The old guy was so busy beating up Baz he didn't see him. Next we heard an old woman screaming, followed by what sounded like bones being broken on impact with a baseball bat, and then the bloke reappeared and raced round the corner in the same direction as Terry's van. The old guy, still piling into Baz with his stick, completely missed it all. Before I knew what to think Terry appeared shouting and screaming at us to get back in the van.

'What about Baz?' shouted Del.

'Don't worry, he'll be fine, just get in,' screamed Terry.

We ran to the van and piled in. Terry was ecstatic.

'You beauties, you lovely little beauties,' he kept saying over and over, in between bouts of hysterical laughter and retching coughs.

I couldn't understand why he seemed to be so happy. I was devastated. Baz had ruined it for me by breaking that bleeding window. As the window had smashed, so had my dreams. Or so I thought; but I was wrong. Very wrong. Very, very wrong. Very, very, very wrong.

'That boy of yours is the best bleeding footballer in the whole bleeding world, Reg,' Terry said to Dad when we got home.

'Really?' said Dad, clearly gobsmacked, not because he hadn't known about my ability, but because Terry never said anything nice about anyone.

I suddenly felt a pang of guilt about Baz.

'I feel a pang of guilt about Baz,' I said to Terry.

'Never heard of him,' snapped Terry, 'and nor have you, get it?'

I nodded with compliance, but later that day I tracked down the hospital where Baz had been admitted and took him that week's issue of *Shoot!* magazine.

'And you know what, mate,' Terry continued saying to Dad. 'Between you and me, I reckon it's time he started playing for the Novas.'

The Novas. Bridgeway Novas. I couldn't believe my tiny, weeny little ears. Bridgeway Novas were legendary. They were the top local lads' football team. They'd won every-thing and even produced some players who'd gone on to play at the top level, such as Charlie Nettlers and Billy Chuzzlenie.

'Yeah,' continued Terry. 'A couple of my associates are very interested in making sure Bridgeway Novas get the results they want. With your boy in the side, I reckon we can give them exactly that, no bother. If they're prepared to pay for it of course.' And then he started laughing again. And coughing, until I couldn't really tell when he'd stopped laughing and started coughing, it was like one, long-drawn-out laugh-cough or cough-laugh.

Even though it was one of the most unpleasant and disgusting sounds on God's earth, I didn't mind. At that moment I was about as happy as any seven-year-old could be. Clearly, in those few short moments outside the post office, Terry had seen enough to know I had what it takes. Sometimes it works out like that. Even though he had absolutely no footballing ability himself, his talent was obviously spotting talent in others. He believed in me and I'll never forget that.

'Bridgeway Novas,' I kept saying to myself as I went upstairs to finally get out of those damp, soggy pyjamas.

It was the start.

I'd arrived.

CHAPTER 3:

Novas' New Star (David Feckham)

'Really? Blimey.'

'If you know what's good for you you'll play the Feckham kid when he needs to be played, all right?'

Uncle Terry had been true to his word. Barely a week after my post office 'trial' he'd taken me and two of his friends to meet the manager of Bridgeway Novas, Stanley Overwood. Sitting outside in the corridor whilst they had their discussions I was so tense it seemed as if time was standing still, much as if it was playing a game of Statues or Sleeping Lions. Either that or my watch had stopped.

From inside the room I could make out snippets of conversation followed by what sounded like furniture being hastily moved around; I fathomed that Stanley also needed some removals doing and that was why Terry had brought his friends along, to help him with that and thus smooth my passage into the Novas. Either way it worked and before too long Uncle Terry called for me to enter the room.

'Stanley here's got something to say to you,' he said. 'Isn't that right, Stanley?'

Stanley, who was suffering from a nasty nosebleed at the time, stepped forward. 'Welcome to the Novas,' he said holding out his unbloodied, and, as I was later to discover, unbroken hand.

From that moment on my young life was dominated by the

Novas. Stanley was a legend round our way. He'd taken the club from nothing to something via anything. He had very clear ideas about how to manage a football team and he went about things the right way. He was like a father to us lads, not just because of the way he cared for us, but because he was sleeping with most of our mothers on the side as well.

At home all I could talk about were the Novas. It was Novas this, Novas that, Novas in, Novas out, Novas shake it all about. Of course no one was interested in me so I mainly talked to myself, but that was okay. I was a good listener.

We trained twice a week at the local park and from day one I knew this was a proper outfit, run like a professional football team. Not only were they well organised with all the right kit, but they also made sure we got a real feel for the game by ensuring there was lots of banter, mickey-taking and practical joking. Well, it's part and parcel isn't it? The pranks, the changing-room antics. Even when I was playing at a much higher level, for The Schnitzel and Parrot in the South by South East Manchester Pub Sunday League Division 4 (North), there'd be a few practical jokes before a game: like the time the other players all dampened their towels, spun them round and round until they were like whips and then used them to flick at my legs, arms, head and any other exposed part of my body until they drew blood. It was hilarious.

At the Novas the jokes came thick and fast. From the moment I arrived the other lads gave me the cold shoulder treatment. During training, on the way home and even when we were playing matches, not a single soul would talk to me, or look at me, unless they were momentarily distracted by a passing bird and found that I was in their eye line. It went on for the first six weeks and still makes me laugh when I think about it today. It didn't bother me at all; in fact, I was honoured to have been singled out for such 'special' treatment.

It did have a side effect though. At the time my heroes were the likes of Bryan Robson, Ray 'Butch' Wilkins, Gordon 'Gordon' McQueen and Arnold Muhren from the Manchester United team back then. I knew that one day I might meet them, play on the same team as them even, but at seven, that seemed a long way off. So I did what a lot of kids used to do and made them into my imaginary friends.

It was great; the five of us were like a little gang. Okay, so like any bunch of lads there'd be the occasional falling out, and from time to time one or other of them would be not talking to me, but on the whole we were the best of friends. I can still remember some of our conversations today.

BUTCH: All right, David mate, how's it going?
ME: I'm very well thank you for asking Butch. How are you?
BUTCH: Fine, David.
ME: Great. And how are you Bryan?
BRYAN: I'm very well.
ME: That's brilliant. And how are you Gordon?
GORDON: Och aye the noo I'm very well. (Because he was Scottish see?)
ME: Fantastic. And what about you Arnold, how are you?
ARNOLD: Oh yesh, I'm alsho fine. (Because he was Dutch.)

I still talk to them today sometimes, but it's not the same. I guess I just don't have the same imagination that I had as a kid. Perhaps, when he's a little older, Chorlton-Cum-Hardy will have some imaginary friends and I can introduce him to my imaginary friends. They might even become friends themselves, my imaginary friends and his imaginary friends, who knows?

After six weeks I knew that the joking had come to an end. Stanley came up to me, his nose bleeding again for some reason, and said, 'David, you're in the team, you're playing this Sunday.'

To say I was gobsmacked was the understatement of the year. It was more like a whole flotilla of juggernauts had driven headlong into my mouth.

'This is it, Bryan, this is it,' I said.

'What?' said Stanley. 'My name's Stanley, you stupid little shit. Who the fuck is Bryan?'

In my excitement I'd forgotten that my imaginary friends were imaginary and instead of talking to them in my head I'd spoken out loud. I started to explain to Stanley, but he was gone. It didn't bother me though. I was in the team, that was all that mattered.

The game in question was a home match against Barnham Green Common. Traditionally matches between the two of us had always been a bit tasty; we hated them and they hated us. Or the other way round, I forget now. None of us knew why we hated each other though, we just did, and this game was no different.

That season Barnham were by far and away the worst team in the league with a grand total of no points from their first five fixtures. Bridgeway Novas on the other hand had made a cracking start to the season, winning all of their games and conceding no goals. I hadn't played yet, but that was clearly because Stanley was holding his best players back until later in the season when the pitches would be heavier. Using me for this particular game was slightly confusing therefore; the only reason I could think of was that some scouts must be coming to watch us and he wanted them to see me.

The day of the game proved me right. In the changing room before kick-off my head was full of whats and ifs and maybes and perhapses and who knowses and could bes and well that's a possibilities and could happens. My little mind was buzzing, I was furiously chatting away to all the guys in my 'gang', apart from Gordon who had the hump with me at the time. In fact they were so talkative I barely heard Stanley's team talk. It didn't matter though, because just after it, Uncle Terry came in and gave me a little team talk all of my own.

'Right, listen up,' he said. 'There are some very important people here today, who'll be watching you very closely. So I want you to get involved, son, in everything. Forget your position, I want you in defence, midfield, attack, even in bleedin' goal if needs be. Got that?'

I nodded so much that the imaginary guys in my head got dizzy. It made me realise how much this game meant to Terry and, running out on to the pitch, I was determined not to let him down.

There were loads of people there. As well as all the mums and dads who usually watched us, apart from mine, Terry had brought all his mates along. Incredibly they were all just as supportive as he was. They spent the whole game shouting at me to get in there and chase the ball. Which is exactly what I did. Every single one. By half time I was so exhausted my little legs felt like jelly with pieces of tinned fruit in them. Incredibly the score was still nil–nil though.

The second half followed much the same pattern, but somehow we couldn't break them down. Then, with only a couple of minutes left, and completely against the run of play, they got a free kick on the edge of the box. Amazingly, Stanley, whose nose had started bleeding again, told me to go in goal. It was a very unorthodox move, but then that was Stanley all over: when the chips were down he'd pull out all the stops and pick the chips up again.

The Barnham players crowded into our penalty box. I had a quick check and spotted one who wasn't marked.

'Craig,' I shouted to Craig, our left back. 'Pick up their number seven.'

But Craig couldn't hear me, so I had a decision to make. Leave their number seven free or leave the goal free. I knew that split-second decisions like that one could have a huge effect on the outcome of a game and I had to make the right choice.

I moved out of the goal and picked up Barnham's number seven myself, sticking close to him even when he ran out to the corner spot. Unfortunately it turned out to be the wrong decision because instead of playing the ball to him, the kick-taker went for goal. I turned to see the ball nestling in the back of our net and the Barnham boys doing their traditional goal celebration dance, a choreographed routine that involved tutus, ballet shoes and face paints.

There was no time for us to get an equaliser. As the ref blew the final whistle I was pretty sure we had lost, though I did ask him just to be sure. I was right. One–nil to Barnham. The changing room afterwards was like a morgue, everyone was freezing cold and lying flat on their backs on stone slabs, not moving. No one was blaming me, though, which was a testament to how much we were a team. And anyway, who's to say what might have happened if I hadn't marked their number seven, something which Craig should have been doing? If it was anyone's fault, which it wasn't because, as I've made clear, we were a team and didn't single anyone out for blame, it was Craig's. Yes Craig would definitely have taken the rap if blame was being apportioned (which it wasn't).

Not blaming Craig wasn't the main thing on my mind though. I was more concerned about Uncle Terry and his mates, the scouts. Would they take my whole performance into account or would the 'goal' incident, that was bloody Craig's fault, colour their opinion of me?

After showering, covering myself in talcum powder from head to foot and then showering again, I dressed and walked out to find out what my reception was going to be.

'There he is,' shouted Terry as soon as I set foot outside the changing rooms. 'Son, you mental bastard, you were fucking great. Here.'

He pressed something into my hand. It was a two-pence piece. I couldn't believe it. I'd never seen so much money in my life and Terry was giving it to me. It said so much.

For the rest of that season I played intermittently for the Novas. Whenever there was a big game I'd naturally get the nod, but it was a tall order. I couldn't turn things on and off like a tap, or the on/off switch on a telly, so we never quite managed to win one of those games. It didn't bother me as Uncle Terry always seemed pleased with my overall performances, but what I needed was a decent run in the team.

At the end of the season I got my chance. We'd finished second in the league after narrowly losing the crunch game on the last day of the season. I'd played and played well, but felt my third own goal should have been disallowed for ungentlemanly conduct after our goalie, Barry Pratt, had shouted, 'Oi, it's the second half now, we've changed ends, we're kicking the other way you twat,' at me.

The ref missed it though and gave the goal, something he wouldn't have done if they'd had audio refereeing. This is something of a bugbear of mine and probably stems from that game. It really pisses me off the way people go on about video refereeing all the time, using cameras to help make decisions about whether a ball crossed the line or not. What's needed are highly sensitive boom mikes, carefully positioned round the pitch, the sort that could hear a pin drop or someone whispering obscenities under their breath eight miles away. That way all manner of dissent and ungentlemanly conduct, that goes unpunished, would be picked up and dealt with properly.

One of the best things about the Novas were the trips we used to have. Stanley had literally thousands of pen pals so was able to organise for us to play in tournaments all over the world. Over the years we went to Ulan Bator, Ouagadougou, Wollongong and Redcar. But that first year we went to the best place in the world as far as I was concerned: Manchester. Yes Manchester, home of Manchester United. And Manchester City. And to a lesser extent Rochdale, Wigan and Bolton.

This was my big chance. Even though most of their supporters came from London, not many United scouts found their way down there. Now I would be playing on their very doorstep and they wouldn't be able to miss me.

There were sixteen teams in the tournament: fifteen from various locations around the UK, and one from Chad. We were split into four groups of four with the top two from each progressing into a knockout quarter-final stage. With Maths not being my best subject I couldn't figure that out, but I guessed if we just kept winning we'd be okay.

Uncle Terry and his mates couldn't make the tournament. Business seemed to be going well for them and they'd all gone for a well-deserved break on the Costa del Sol. Before he left, though, Terry had been kind enough to tell me that he'd had a word with Stanley and I'd be playing in every game. I nearly cried when he told me that, but didn't because I was a boy, and because I'd had my tear ducts removed when I was three.

For most of the lads the tournament was really a bit of fun, a chance to relax at the end of a long season, which is probably why they dispensed with our usual strip for the games and wore loud, colourful Hawaiian shirts, Bermuda shorts and sunglasses. But not me. In the days before we left I practised as much as I could. I worked day and night on my skills and fitness, as well as my fitness and skills. Mum, Dad and the girls also helped with my preparations. Knowing that I might find it difficult being on my own away from home, they all went on holiday a week before the tournament started, thus helping me simulate the isolation, homesickness and loneliness I was expecting to feel. It helped a great deal because, even though we all lodged with families once we were up there, within a very short space of time mine spent practically every waking hour out, and most of the sleeping hours as well. Thank goodness for my imaginary friends. Or to be more precise, friend – Butch was the only one left, the others having all become imaginary friends to other lads.

To be honest I don't remember all that much about the tournament. Playing in every game really took its toll on me, especially as by the third game a lot of my team-mates had taken to relaxing in deckchairs for the duration of the ninety minutes. I didn't mind though, it gave me a chance to really shine, something I'm sure I would have done if the lads hadn't kept asking me to fetch them ice cream and cold drinks (even though everyone knows on a hot day you should drink hot drinks to cool you down!).

One of the games, though, I'll never forget. It was our final group game. Unfortunately we'd lost the other two by the narrowest of margins, 8–0 and 14–0. We were beaten in the first because our centre forward Tony pitched his deckchair in an offside position, which meant our opponents got a free kick whenever I was in on goal.

The second game followed a similar pattern, though personally I'd argue that Tony's chair was level with the last defender and thus he was onside, but that's the rub of the green for you; sometimes you get those decisions, sometimes you don't.

For the final game we were up against Ashton Park Wednesday North End Athletic United Wanderers Academicals, who counted amongst their number a young, scrawny-looking lad with fair hair and hazel brown eyes. He looked a bit useful and I knew from the off that if we were to get anything out of this game, I would have to win a personal battle with him. So I employed a tactic known as man-for-man marking. It's very complex and was originally developed in Italy at a time when their leagues would often go for three, maybe even four seasons without a goal being scored in any of the games. To simplify it enormously, what it means is that wherever the person you're marking goes, you go. You stick to them like glue. And not the crap glue you get at school, Gloy I think it was called, the sort that couldn't stick anything to anything. Or Pritt Stick. Or Uhu. Or even Bostik. You stick to them like superglue, the sort that is so strong it can stick your fingers together, if you've got a bit on your fingers and you hold them together for long enough.

I went everywhere this lad went and it worked. If I remember correctly I restricted him to only one or two goals. Or maybe nine. But the important thing is that I was noticed. Clearly word of my performances in the previous two games had got around and for this last one, there they were, scouts.

There were three of them and I was pretty sure they were from Manchester United. They watched everything I did, and everything this other lad did too of course, but that was only because I was sticking so close to him and in order to watch me they inevitably had to watch him. It made me that much more determined, in fact probably two, maybe even three times more determined, that's how much more determined it made me.

When the ref blew his whistle for full time we both knew we'd been in a right old battle and, still marking him very tightly, I did what footballers have been doing for centuries. I offered him my shirt.

'Urrgh, fuck off, it's all sweaty,' he said. 'I don't want that horrible smelly piece of shit.'

I looked at my shirt. He was right, it was drenched in sweat.

'Sorry mate,' I said. 'By the way, my name's David, David Feckham. You played well.'

'David Feckham? Are you taking the living piss?'

'No mate, why?'

'My name's David Beckham, that's why.'

'Really? Blimey.' I was stunned.

'So you're really called David Feckham?'

'Yeah. And you're really called David Beckham?'

'Yeah.'

There was a moment when we both looked at each other and then we pissed ourselves laughing. It felt great, but unfortunately that's when I lost him. Whilst I was rolling about on the floor in hysterics, he must have wandered off. You see that's the thing about man for man marking, you can't take your eyes off the geezer you're marking for a second, even once the game's over. Next thing I know he's surrounded by scouts and I can't get near him or them. Of course, but for that one mistake the scouts would have been talking to me and not him, they'd have had to because I would have been marking him so tightly. It was a tough lesson to learn, but then if you enrol in the school of hard knocks you've got to expect the knocks to be hard.

I was a bit dejected walking away from the ground, but then I looked up and saw him.

'Becks,' I shouted.

'Fecks,' he shouted back.

I trotted over to where he was.

'Those scouts interested in you then?' I said, desperately trying to sound nonchalant, but actually sounding jealous, bitter, envious and full of hate.

'Yeah, yeah,' he said, genuinely sounding nonchalant. 'They want to meet my mum and dad and see about me doing some training at the club.'

'Great, great,' I said, venom spitting out of me with every word.

'I'm sure I'll be seeing you again then.'

'Yeah, with a name like yours I'll definitely be looking out for you.'

'Yeah, yeah, I'll race you to the England team. First to get there buys the other one a Coke.'

'You're on, mate. See you around.'

Then he was gone. Whatever happened, I knew our paths were bound to cross again.

The next few seasons with the Novas passed in a blur of excitement and puberty. In fact at one stage I thought I might need glasses, but it was more of a metaphorical blur than a real one. As my young body developed, so did my footballing skills. Of course I don't mean that my footballing skills grew pubic hair; more that I was growing into the footballer I was going to become.

I continued to play intermittently, whenever Stanley felt that my particular skills were needed, usually in a big game that we really had to win. More often than not we didn't win them, well, we never did, but somehow it didn't seem to matter, other than to Stanley and all the other lads and their parents. What was important was team spirit. Every-one got on really well, or so they told me after the parties they used to have that I didn't go to because our phone was always on the blink and the post was crap.

When I was thirteen my life changed for ever. It was at the end of the '86/87 season. We'd had our best year ever and were in contention for the title, though unfortunately due to injury I hadn't played much. I sprained my Achilles heel in training early on. It's a very common injury and according to our physio, Les, even though there's abso-lutely no pain and no noticeable manifestations, it can be extremely damaging to carry on playing with it. Uncle Terry was also away a lot that year, his work on the Costa was keeping him busy, but he made an extra-special effort to come over for that game, changing his name and getting a new passport just so he could be there for me.

We were up against Dynamo Dollis Hill. The two of us were level on points at the top of the league, but we had a marginally better goal difference so only needed a draw to become champions. I knew it was exactly the sort of game that, under normal circumstances, Stanley would pick me to play in, but I wasn't a hundred per cent sure my Achilles heel had cleared up. I needn't have worried though. At the club on the day of the game, Les came up and kicked me really hard in the heel.

'Did that hurt?' he said.

'Yes, yes, ow, yes,' I said in between gasps of intense agony.

'Good. Then you're cured.'

So I was in.

There was a great atmosphere that day, which if I remem-ber correctly was slightly overcast and drizzly, though remembering incorrectly it was sunny and dry. Loads of people turned up for the match. Dollis Hill brought quite a large contingent of fans and we had plenty of support. Uncle Terry and his mates were there, or rather, Uncle Percival and his mates, and even Dad came along for it.

Before kick-off Stanley gathered us all together for the team talk. The excitement must have got to him because he had a wild stare in his eyes.

'I don't care any more, I just don't care,' he said. 'They can cut my balls off if they want and feed them to the ducks, but we ain't losing this game, right lads?'

He said all of this looking directly at me and I knew that what he was really saying was, 'David, we're relying on you, don't let us down.'

The game was played at a frantic pace. I was all over the shop and there was even a few niggles, mainly between me and my team-mates, but that happens when there's so much at stake. It was only nerves and they can make you do funny things like tackle your own player when he has the ball, something that happened to me on many occasions during the first half.

At the break the score was still nil–nil, but that was about to change. Dollis Hill kicked off for the second half and booted the ball straight to me.

'Dave, over here mate,' shouted our left back Andy.

As far as I was concerned his shout had come from behind me, so I turned and lofted a glorious pass to him. Unfortunately, my hearing had been playing tricks on me, and he was in fact standing a few feet to my right. If he had been standing on our goal line, the ball I'd just played would have been perfect. Instead it sailed past our goalie and into the net. Football can be a cruel game at times, and that was one of those. Andy was gutted at having caused the goal.

The rest of the second half we piled on the pressure, but

they were a tough nut to crack and we just didn't have the right nutcrackers. In the last minute of the game, though, we got a corner. Everyone went up for it, even our keeper, which I thought was silly seeing as how he'd left the goal empty.

'Get back in goal,' I shouted at him.

'Get lost mate, this is our last chance, I'm staying here,' he said.

I couldn't believe it. The red mist descended and I'm sorry to say I swung for him. Luckily he ducked and I fell forward. Incredibly my falling forward coincided exactly with the ball coming in from the corner. It hit me full on the forehead and flew into the back of the net. A perfect diving header.

For a moment there was silence. Then everyone on our team jumped up in the air for joy. They were ecstatic. To a man they ran to congratulate Alan, who had taken the corner.

It was literally the last kick/head of the game. We had got the draw and were champions at last. I couldn't believe it. I ran over to where Dad and Uncle Percival were.

'Now then,' Uncle Percival was saying. 'You've been good to me so I'm going to be good to you. You have twenty-four hours. If you're not gone by then, you will have made the biggest mistake of your life. Got that?'

Terry was clearly telling him that now was the time for me to move on and up, to bigger and better things. Dad nodded furiously, then turned to look at me. He was so happy he couldn't even get any words out, he just stared.

The following morning I knew I was right. I awoke to find the house empty and everyone and everything gone. They'd gone on ahead of me.

Mum, bless her, had left me a note. It read, 'David, get the fuck out of there as fast as you can before they come round and get you. Go to Uncle Cedric and Aunt Delia's place, you'll be safe there.'

Reading between and above and below the lines I knew exactly what she meant. I was headed for Cedric and Delia's place. In Manchester. Home of Manchester United. (And as I've said before Manchester City and to a lesser extent Bolton, Wigan and Rochdale.)

CHAPTER 4:

Manchester, England, England, Great Britain

'Lacrosse?'

As the train pulled into Manchester Piccadilly, I smiled and tipped the woman pushing the peanut trolley. I disembarked and hurried through the gate.

The concourse was empty except for two teenage health freaks furtively consuming a multi-pack of Nutrigrain bars. I checked the contents of my wallet: four pounds and twenty-three pence. I cursed myself for tipping the peanut trolley woman and ambled outside. The grey Manchester skyline looked particularly grey that day, and as a couple of birds flew overhead, I could have sworn I heard them laughing. This instantly cheered me up. Laughing birds! This was going to be an even crazier adventure than I'd imagined.

I found a large timetable screwed to a bus stop. I scanned it for a possible route but noticed the small print at the bottom: *This timetable is for transport staff only. The public shouldn't be able to make head or tail of it.* I nodded with appreciation and flagged down the number 43.

The bus I got was driven by a young lad. I started chatting to him and asked him his age. He told me he was eighteen, but when I peeked inside his holdall, his schoolbooks revealed he was in fact ten. That's the city of Manchester for you: progressive.

After a twenty-minute white-knuckle ride, our youthful driver did a 360-degree spin and swerved the vehicle to stop directly outside my aunt and uncle's house. This was some feat as they lived on the fifth floor of a tower block. He wished me luck and sped off over a balustrade.

I knocked on the door three times and waited.

Nothing.

I knocked again three times.

Still nothing.

I sighed and, reaching down into my rucksack, pulled out the police enforcer that Dad had given me in case I ever got locked out of the house. (He'd got a gross off a bent copper from Chigwell.) The one downside of carrying this piece of equipment was that when you used it you had to shout 'POLICE! POLICE! DON'T MOVE! WE KNOW YOU'RE IN THERE!'

I crunched the enforcer against the wooden door frame and it splintered into a thousand pieces. I yelled out the entry phrase and strode in. Aunt Delia, Uncle Cedric, First Cousin Barry (8) and First Cousin Emma (6) were all watching TV in the lounge. It was some programme where they try to feed Chris Tarrant to a pride of lions in the Australian outback and he can only be spared if three C-list celebrities manage to makeover a mediaeval castle in four hours, using only sacked postal workers as assistants.

'Hi everyone!' I said, bursting into the room.

'Shut it!' chorused the entire family. 'This is the bit where Tarrant gets it.'

I understood their commitment to the show. Mum had told me that Delia had once spent a whole year's shopping budget on phone calls to premium-rate aspiring quiz contestant phone lines. So, I sat down on the edge of

Cedric's armchair and watched with them in silence. Tarrant made a last-minute escape disguised as a rare orchid and the family tried to contain their disappointment.

Barry and Emma had an argument about what to watch next. He wanted bare-knuckle rabbit fighting live from Glasgow city centre. She wanted to catch *Destroying Perfectly Healthy Houses* in which builders choose structurally sound residences to demolish and then rebuild them according to how viewers had voted.

After five minutes of this row, Cedric said he'd had enough and threw the telly at me. I ducked and it crashed into a wall, its indent fashioning some handy shelves. He then turned to face me.

'David,' he said, reaching out his hand.

I flushed with warmth. This was the welcome I'd been waiting for. After all he was my Dad's only brother.

I held out my hand to shake it, but he pulled a face.

'Your rent?' he asked.

'Oh yeah,' I said fumbling in my pocket. 'I'm a tiny bit skint at the minute,' I explained, holding out three pound coins.

Uncle Cedric looked across at Aunt Delia and then back at me.

'All right,' he said gruffly. 'Until you start earning up here, you're on a strictly bed and breakfast tariff. When the cash starts to flow in, we'll move you to half-board.'

I nodded earnestly, even though the last thing on my mind was working and earning money. I was desperate to ask about the local football scene, but realised that now wasn't a great moment. *Give yourself time to settle in*, I instructed myself, *then go for it*.

'Let me show you your room, David,' said Aunt Delia, getting off the sofa and stubbing out the four cigarettes she simultaneously had on the go. I followed her down a narrow corridor at the end of which she pulled open a door to reveal an airing cupboard.

'Sorry, love,' she said tutting, and pulled open another door. This led to a room that actually was a shoebox.

'What do you think?' she asked.

'Is the airing cupboard free?' I asked.

It took some time to get my stuff organised in my new room. The boiler was one of those giant affairs and made any quick movements unadvisable. But I could see one great advantage of the space. It was bloody warm in there. I smiled to myself as I thought about cosy evenings spent in my room defying the cruelty of the biting Manchester winds.

At five-thirty, Aunt Delia called me into the kitchen. There was a delicious smell coming from a pan on the hob. There were five bowls lined up on the side and I nodded with silent appreciation. This really was a home from home. Aunt Delia began to serve and the intoxicating aroma wafted across the room as she placed the bowls in front of us.

'It's stewed apples,' she said helpfully when she noticed my slightly bemused expression.

I smiled up at her.

'I love stewed apples!' I said appreciatively, immediately deciding that maybe this was a common first course for a Manchester tea.

And they were fantastic. Really creamy. Granny Smiths lovingly mashed into puréed heaven.

I polished my portion off and winked at First Cousin Barry.

He scowled back and drew a finger across his throat.

Delia was on her feet again, clearing up the plates and hovering over another pot that she'd pulled out of the oven. She started serving on to five clean plates.

I was the first to be served.

'It's stewed apples,' she said helpfully when she noticed my slightly bemused expression.

'Right,' I said, managing another smile.

The same happened with dessert.

'It's stew—'

'Yes Auntie Delia, I've got it. It's stewed apples.'

I finished my third portion and wiped my lips with a napkin.

She beamed at me. 'What a good lad,' she noted with pleasure and offered me seconds.

'I'm fine thanks Auntie,' I grimaced, 'I just need to visit the toilet.'

Okay David, I said to myself as I sat on the bog. *They like stewed apples. That's fine. Many people like stewed apples. BUT NO ONE HAS IT FOR ALL THREE FUCKING COURSES! Maybe it's a Manchester thing? Just sit tight and keep smiling.*

As the clock struck six, Uncle Cedric disappeared and came back a few seconds later. He threw my parka at me.

'Come on, David, we're heading out.'

I stood up and slipped my coat on.

'See you later,' he nodded at the three members of his family still seated at the table.

It was a chilly night and I pulled my coat tightly round myself as we walked along the dimly lit streets. After five minutes I spotted a small arc of yellowy-orange light on a street corner.

As we got nearer and nearer to this light source I could make out the words clinging to the fluttering sign: The Schnitzel and Parrot.

With every step now, Uncle Cedric was getting more and more excited.

'This, young David, is my refuge. It's my oasis of peace in a world gone mad.'

I sensed that my uncle might be something of a philosopher and racked my brains for a witty quip from Rousseau or a gem of insight from Gramsci.

'Is that your local?' I finally said.

He looked sideways at me and nodded with pride.

'Oh yes,' he replied, rubbing his hands together, 'oh yes.'

He pushed the pub door open confidently and we walked inside.

The place was heaving. There must have been a couple of hundred people in a space designed for seventy, maximum. And I saw straight away that Uncle Cedric was like royalty in there. It felt like everybody knew his name and they were always glad he came.

The barman, a great hulk of a Geordie called Spike, clapped his hands on spying Uncle Cedric.

'My finest customer!' he yelled with delight, doing a mock bow to my uncle. My uncle bowed back.

'And who might this young lad be?' grinned Spike, embedding a long finger deeply into my right cheek.

'This here is my one and only nephew,' shouted Uncle Cedric. 'Say hello to David, everyone.'

There were a few murmurs and a couple of nods.

'I SAID SAY HELLO TO DAVID, EVERYONE!'

It was as if Uncle Cedric had lit the touchpaper.

'HELLO DAVID!' roared the entire pub in a perfect four-part barbershop-style harmony.

'All right,' I nodded.

Uncle Cedric tugged at my arm. 'What are you having, son?'

'I'll just have a Coke,' I replied.

'For God's sake lad – you're twelve now. It's a real drink or nothing. That's four pints for me, Spike and a half of vodka for the lad,' bellowed Uncle Cedric.

Spike disappeared and returned a couple of minutes later

with the drinks. Uncle Cedric put his hand into his pocket and I watched, waiting for him to pull out a fistful of cash. But instead he pulled out a small purple and green strip of plastic.

I was impressed.

'There's not many pubs back home that take credit cards,' I said to Uncle Cedric and Spike.

'That's no Visa,' explained Uncle Cedric.

'It's his Pub Loyalty Card,' added Spike. 'At the minute he's the only customer who drinks enough to merit one, but we're thinking of adding a few more regulars and if that goes well, the brewery are thinking about going national.'

'How does it work?' I asked.

Uncle Cedric grinned. 'Every ten pints I drink, I get a free pint. If I drink more than a hundred in a week, I get two free shorts. I get a bill at the end of each month. I could pay by cheque, but there's a handling charge so I do it by direct debit. It's far easier and more economic that way.'

By now, the entire pub was silent, listening to my uncle's speech.

Spike looked around the room.

'Get on with your drinking!' he yelled and immediately the general hubbub returned.

And from that moment on, I felt totally at home with Spike and the other drinkers at The Schnitzel and Parrot. I went there every night with Uncle Cedric and it became part of the fabric of my life in Manchester, the *Lycra* if you will. It was all part of my transition from boyhood to early manhood. After closing time, I'd stagger down the road, totally sober, with the full weight of a bladdered Uncle Cedric on my shoulder.

Some nights it was a miracle that I ever got him back to the flat. Aunt Delia had got sick and tired of waiting up and bollocking him, so she'd had a cardboard cutout of herself made, complete with angry expression and wagging finger. It worked a treat. Every time Uncle Cedric saw this 2-D representation of his long-suffering spouse, he begged for forgiveness, started sobbing and sang all the songs from *Mary Poppins*. This worked brilliantly until he got to 'Supercalafragilisticexpialidocious'.

Each night, I finally dropped him on to the sofa at about one a.m. and sloped off to the airing cupboard to get some much-needed kip.

It was a great life but it was football I'd come to Manchester for.

At the end of my first week, I plucked up the courage and told Uncle Cedric about my passion.

He listened intently and spoke when I'd finished.

'Lacrosse?' he said.

'No, Uncle Cedric, football.'

'Oh football,' he nodded. 'The Schnitzel and Parrot have a whole football set-up. I'll speak to Spike.'

Before we set off for the pub that night, Uncle Cedric said to Aunt Delia, 'We're going to be seeing an awful lot less of David from now on. He's going to be joining a football team.'

Aunt Celia was devastated by this news but managed to mask her sadness by pulling her jumper over her head and sliding on her knees across the lounge carpet shouting 'YESSSSS!'

And he was true to his word. That night, he asked Spike if I could play for the pub's junior side. Spike looked at the huge line of pints resting in front of Uncle Cedric on the bar.

'He could play for Brazil if I was the manager,' roared Spike, 'you're my best customer, Cedric. Of course he can. I'll speak to Frank. He might be the manager but if he doesn't do what I want, he'll be managing nomarks in the lower leagues faster than a cheetah on rocket-powered roller blades. Just leave it with me.'

I was ecstatic. I hugged Uncle Cedric. He hugged Spike. Spike hugged his wife Kelly. Kelly threw Spike head first over the bar.

That night, I dragged Uncle Cedric home at breakneck speed. I'd nailed two planks of wood to these four large pallets. It was a kind of sleigh and it helped me get Cedric home in less than an hour.

When we got in that night, I was so over-excited that I spent two hours pacing the flat and talking to the cardboard cutout of Delia.

That Sunday was my first practice and I had to force myself not to get there too early. When the first lads began to arrive, they nodded at me. By eleven, the whole squad was there. The junior team coach was a right hard bastard called Frank Tallon. He asked for silence when we were out on the tarmac.

'Listen up everyone,' he called. 'That new kid is called David Feckham. He's from London. As he's from the smoke, he probably really reckons himself so your job is to break his spirit. If he can handle that, then he'll fit in just perfectly.'

Four lads who looked as if they were physically stuck together legged it over in my direction.

'We're Miggsy, Puttsy, Brevilley and Scooby,' they said together.

'What's the gaffer like?' I asked.

'He's a wanker,' they said.

'Oi you lot. Shut it!' hissed Frank.

'You're not wrong there lads,' I said to the foursome.

Frank spat in my direction and continued his warm-up chat.

I have to admit that Frank's training was tough. He regularly took us to the Manchester Ship Canal and made us do press-ups in the putrid waters. On more than one occasion, a couple of lads got hit by a barge. But Frank was a lifetime member of the British Waterways Board and was able to keep these incidents out of the papers.

And to make matters worse, he continually picked on me. He could clearly see that I was a cut above the rest and so was especially hard on me.

But even though I knew why he was doing it, one day I lost my rag with him.

'Why are you always having a go at me?' I demanded in the changing room.

Frank glared at me. 'If you don't know by now you'll never know.'

Following our little chat things got a lot better. After all of my years in football, I've learnt that sometimes the right word, in the right ear, from the right mouth, in the right room, with the right curtains, at the right time, is all it takes to defuse a situation.

After that incident, Frank stopped hassling me and once or twice let me do the team talks at half time.

The Schnitzel and Parrot junior side played in the North West Sector 7 Junior Pub League and it was Frank's lifetime ambition to win the title. He'd tried to achieve this in so many ways. His first approach had been to try to produce a top quality team. When that failed, he'd tried playing with 'ringers' – local professionals whom no one had heard of yet. But they insisted on big money and free trips to Menorca, so he had to stop employing them. He then attempted to threaten the other managers, but they were all much harder than him and were more likely to inflict damage on him than vice versa.

So it was up to us to do the right thing for the boss. As with the Novas, I didn't get that many games, but when everyone else (including Frank's wife) was injured, I got the call. I played every match as if my life depended on it.

There was one game against Sneath Salford, on a blustery Sunday afternoon in January, where I could see that their centre forward was going to embark on a mazy run past five of our players and then score with a ferocious, swerving volley. I knew there was only one thing to do. I ran to our goal line, pushed our keeper, 'Selby', out of the way and pulled down our goal, stanchions, posts and all. As soon as their centre forward looked up to unleash his shot he discovered there was nothing to aim at. This led to all of their players chasing me round the pitch, screaming ancient curses at me. The ref abandoned the game and called for a Securicor van to escort me home. We were docked three league points. Everyone connected with our team pretended to be furious with me, but I knew their game only too well. Loyalty has many faces.

Miggsy, Puttsy, Brevilley and Scooby were always a rock of support for me in the Schnitzel and Parrot junior side. We used to spend a lot of time together when we weren't training. We hung out at this one particular pool club that sold extra-strong lemonade. I wasn't bad at pool, but Puttsy was the best. He could do every trick in the book, including one ingenious affair where he played a shot from the building next door.

They're the sort of mates that everyone needs. Rock solid. I'm particularly fond of Scooby but the fact that he hardly ever speaks means our conversations are a bit one-sided.

Over the next couple of seasons, I settled really well at Uncle Cedric and Aunt Delia's place. Uncle Cedric hadn't mentioned the rent thing again, although First Cousin Barry was often in my room nicking small change.

So when Aunt Delia called me into the kitchen one Monday morning, and pointed to a postcard lying on the kitchen table, my heart sang a madrigal with excitement. I picked it up and turned it over.

> *Dear David*
> *They haven't caught up with us.*
> *We're still alive.*
> *But don't try and find us.*
> *We're all fine and well fed.*
> *Mum, Dad, Clare and Katie.*

I chuckled to myself over their biting sense of irony.

'Are you all right?' asked Delia.

'Never been better,' I smiled, 'never been better.'

At the age of sixteen I met my first proper girlfriend at The Schnitzel and Parrot. I noticed her hanging out with some mates by the cigarette machine, cadging a fag from every punter who purchased a pack. She had spiky blonde hair and was wearing a black leather jacket and brown leather trousers. I thought this showed good initiative (not the trousers, the ciggies) and approached her to talk about various government-sponsored enterprise schemes, but completely forgot what I was going to say when I got to within a couple of feet of her.

I was slightly bowled over by her attractiveness and suddenly felt nervous. What the hell was I thinking of? I was in a strange city, in a strange coat, with a strange relative. She wouldn't go near me.

But Donna proved me wrong. As soon as I'd sheepishly introduced myself, she clapped her hands together.

'A cockney!' she cried. 'A genuine cockney.'

From that moment on I was flavour of the month in Donna's world. Her and her mates Tara and Stella had never met a real Londoner before and it was as if they'd just won the jackpot in a national oddments competition.

Within ten minutes, the three of them had me playing the spoons and singing 'The Lambeth Walk' and 'I'm Forever Blowing Bubbles'. The first one went down well with the pub's clientele but the second was a tad foolish as its connection to West Ham United upset several punters. Donna told them to leave me alone and gave me a tender kiss on the cheek.

I smiled and raised my eyebrows. She licked her lips. I ordered some beef and onion ridged crisps. She chose Frazzles.

Tara and Stella smiled at me with encouragement.

'She likes you!' they beamed.

I felt warm inside. Perhaps this move to Manchester was really meant to be. I could explore the contours of my masculinity as well as working on my skills with Frank and the junior pub team.

Donna and I became a firm item and she brought me back a couple of times to meet her parents. They were incredibly friendly and made me feel part of their house. They never allowed me inside but they were overjoyed with my status as a water feature.

My time with Donna was really great, but there was one time when I didn't behave with the moral coda I'd determined for myself.

I was in the pool club one afternoon with the lads, when Donna turned up. I took her outside so we could chat in private. But we were at the age when lads never miss the opportunity to take the piss out of each other. (That time in a man's life starts at about age ten and goes on until death.) I looked up and saw the four of them at the window inside pulling faces at me. Usually I would have found this funny, but my adolescent hormones were racing all over my body and must have taken a wrong turn somewhere because I lost it. With my face as purple as a tie-dye beetroot, I picked up a piece of slate roofing, ran over to Scooby's chopper bike and smashed it to pieces. If he'd been by himself, he would have got to me quicker, but the others slowed him down.

It was fine in the end though. I bought Scooby a new piece of slate roofing.

I still have very fond memories of Donna. She's never sold any stories about me or us to the newspapers. She's tried. Desperately. But they've never been interested.

I found out subsequently that in the two weeks we were together, she cheated on me with a dustman, a farmhand and a trapeze artist. But none of that bothered me.

It was an invigorating part of my life. I had a new identity and a new goal. If I kept on plying my trade for Frank and the pub's junior side, then who knew what might be round the next corner?

CHAPTER 5:

The Schnitzel and Parrot's (senior team) new star (David Feckham again)

'I got conjunctivitis ain't I?'

I noticed him first towards the end of the 94/95 season. I guess he must have been there before, but if he had, I never knew. When I played football I focused one hundred and eighteen per cent on the game, I was blind to everything else. And deaf and dumb. I couldn't even smell or tactilely sense anything beyond the pitch boundaries.

The person in question was Sralex Ferfuson, legendary manager of the senior pub team. If ever there was a person whose reputation went before them, it was him, though thinking about it his reputation must also have gone after him at some point in order for it then to go before him. Either way, that day my sense of peripheral vision (and sound, smell and tactile sensation) came back for a moment, and I saw him standing on the touchline.

'Scooby,' I shouted to Scooby. 'He's here.'

Scooby looked over to the touchline. Being such a quiet bloke he didn't say anything; he was rationing himself to only three words a day at the time. But I could tell from the way he smiled moronically and flapped his hands in the air like Harpo Marx, that he'd clocked Sralex and was excited.

Before long Brevilley, Miggsy and Puttsy came over to see what all the fuss was about.

'Something's definitely up,' said Brevilley.

Brevilley was rarely wrong when he thought something was up, so we all agreed that something was indeed up.

We discussed what that something could be for the next ten minutes; a mistake in hindsight as we were only twenty minutes into the game we were playing in and during the time we were discussing what could be up our opponents scored three times. Frank was not best pleased. Quite the opposite in fact; he was worst pleased.

'What the bloody hell are you lot playing at?' he bellowed at us. 'Sralex is hardly going to pick you for the senior team now is he?'

So that was it. There had been rumours flying around for some time that Sralex was going to let three or four of the senior players go. Well, not let them go exactly. Two were seeking help for alcohol-related problems, one had just had a heart attack and the other was doing time for GBH, ABH and not having a TV licence, but the end product was the same.

Suddenly the game took on a different meaning. What had once been a dismal, mid-table affair was now a dismal mid-table affair with a different meaning. The effect on the five of us was instantaneous. We started playing our little hearts out. In fact I was so determined to be noticed I played my little liver, kidney and spleen out as well. With fifteen minutes to go we'd made up the three goals we'd conceded during our discussions and were pushing for a fourth. It didn't seem to matter that in that time our opponents had scored another five goals, we were playing with tunnel vision, trying to impress only one person.

As the match ended we all gathered round Frank.

'Now then, lads,' he said. 'Some of you may have spotted someone very special watching us today. He wants to have a word. Let's just hope it's not to give any of you the balloon treatment.'

That sent shivers down our backs. Getting the balloon treatment from Mr Ferfuson was just about the worst thing that could happen to a footballer. If you'd had a bad game he'd come right up to you and deliver a right volley. He'd shout and scream uncontrollably, so much so that he'd blow raspberries and spittle would fly all over you, much as if someone was letting the air out of a blown-up balloon in your face. It was something I would get very used to in the coming years, but today the spittle was staying firmly in his mouth. Well, most of it anyway.

'Thanks, Frank,' said Mr Ferfuson. 'Well played today, lads, you really dug in and gave a hundred and ninety-seven per cent. You might not have won an actual victory, but your play was more ethical than theirs and based on sounder philosophical principles so you definitely won a moral victory, which counts for a lot in my book.'

To a boy we beamed. Mr Ferfuson didn't dish out compliments very often, so when he did it meant something, even if we didn't actually have a clue what he was on about.

'You may not have realised it,' he went on, 'but I've been following your progress over the last few years and I think the time has come for some of you to move up and take the next step in your footballing careers.'

A tremor of excitement rippled through the group. I looked at Miggsy and the others. Apart from our first sexual experience, this was the moment we'd all been waiting for.

'I want the following lads to turn up for training with the senior team this Thursday. Scooby, Miggsy, Brevilley, Puttsy and . . .'

I held my breath.

'. . . Fecks.'

I couldn't believe it. I was so happy I continued to hold my breath for another minute and a half.

I was so excited I didn't even bother to shower. I ran all the way to The Schnitzel and Parrot where I found Uncle Cedric slumped on the floor behind the jukebox, covered in sick.

'Uncle Cedric, Uncle Cedric,' I shouted, shaking him violently and dislodging a few diced carrots from his shirt.

When he'd come to I told him my news.

'Fookin great, son,' he slurred. 'Spike ya Geordie bastard, you're a man of your word and so am I. I'll have another five pints of best and three whiskey chasers.'

Days like that are few and far between and writing about it makes me wonder how many days like that Chorlton-Cum-Hardy and King Lear will have in their lives. I know they're both going to be great players. I've been working hard with Chorlton-Cum-Hardy lately. Mainly on his gobbing, which, to be honest, hadn't previously got beyond the dribbling stage, but he's taken to it like a duck to water. Even though he's only four he can already bring up a decent-sized greenie and flob it from one end of the lounge to the other. It makes me so proud.

Funnily enough, around the time I progressed to the senior side, my mate David Beckham broke in to Manchester United's first team as well. I was still as nuts about United as I'd ever been. More so in fact, almost as if I'd been schizophrenic before, recovered a little and now had relapsed and was ten times worse, that's how much more nuts I was about them. Probably.

I went to see United every opportunity I could. Unfortunately, an opportunity hadn't yet arisen, but when and if it did I would definitely take it. Nonetheless I'd followed Becks's career like we agreed. I was pleased for the lad, but couldn't help feeling that, but for my error in not sticking to him like something magnetic to an electro-magnet, it would have been me playing for United and not him. But I was patient, I would be playing with the big boys soon and then I might get to play with even bigger boys and then the biggest boys ever, so things were definitely looking up.

Training with the senior team was a different ball game to training with the junior team. I mean it was still football, but this was football on a different level, a different stratosphere, a different troposphere and a whole different mesosphere. It was quicker, faster, hastier, speedier, more rapid and a lot less slow. Apart from all those differences there was also the size of my new team-mates. I was still quite small and scrawny for my age so each one of them seemed like King Kong standing on the shoulders of the giant out of *Jack and the Beanstalk*.

But that's how it had always been. I'd never been scared of going in with bigger lads. Dad had seen to that from day one by always tackling me with the full force of his nineteen stone, often from behind and with studs showing. He taught me that they may be big on the outside, but they're not necessarily big on the inside and that it's not the size of the dog in the fight, it's the size of the fight in the dog: basically the same two things only one is more literal than the other.

More often than not I'd come home from those training sessions black and blue, and bleeding internally, but it made me the player I am today: a midfield general with a slight limp and none of my own teeth, so I'm not complaining.

I was now playing in the South by South East Manchester Pub Sunday League Division 4 (North). The previous season The Schnitzel and Parrot had narrowly missed out on promotion to Division 2 (there wasn't a Division 3) and big things were expected of us this year.

The first game was against The Bunion and Malt Loaf, a

free house specialising in local real ales such as Old Stinking Shitwater and Crock O' Crap's Really Weird. We were expected to beat them, but we got hammered. My instructions from Mr Ferfuson had been to stick out on the left wing as far away from the play as possible and run in the opposite direction if the ball should come within twenty yards of me; clearly he wanted me to lure away some of their defenders and make use of the space I was in – football's as much about what you do when you haven't got the ball as when you have got it. But by the time we went twenty-seven–nil down I decided to turn things on a bit. I did all the tricks in my repertoire: I kicked the ball forwards, sideways *and* backwards. I kicked it hard and softly, and did what I like to call the Feckham turn, which is a little like the famous Cruyff turn, only I fall on top of the ball and then get up again.

I suppose I was trying to impress, but Mr Ferfuson was not happy about it. He gave me the balloon treatment with extra raspberries afterwards. In fact he gave me the same treatment after every game, every training session, when I saw him in the pub, in the street and once when both our cars were side by side in a traffic jam. I got so used to having his spittle dribbling down my face that after a while I could tell what he'd had for supper the night before.

I didn't mind, though. It was that pattern again, wasn't it? He was pushing me that bit harder, because he knew I was special. And there was another reason as well of course. He had to bring me down to the level of the other lads. In training and in matches, they would often become mesmerised by my skills and stand in open-mouthed disbelief at what I was doing. Mr Ferfuson knew that if he didn't keep my feet firmly on the ground, things might go to my head and I might start getting too big for my boots. It was great management; I owe him an awful lot. If Stanley had been like a stepfather to me at the Novas, Mr Ferfuson was like a much stricter stepfather and I really appreciated that.

It wasn't till October of that season that things started taking off for us as a team. That was when Canton Erica returned. He'd been missing presumed dead after getting caught in some trawler nets whilst out fishing for fish – herring, sprat and the like. Apparently he'd fallen overboard whilst trying to shoo some seagulls away from the back of the boat.

He was legendary round our way and round many other ways as well, so it was no surprise when he simply strolled into the pub with his heavily starched shift cuffs protruding well beyond his hands, as was his custom both on and off the pitch. Had it been anyone else we would probably have thought it was a ghost or a zombie, but this geezer was something else; returning from the dead was a piece of cake for him.

'Good to see you, Canton,' said Uncle Cedric. 'Drink?'

'Why not?' said the great man.

Twenty minutes later he was completely naked and performing an aria from one of Rigaletto's lesser-known operettas whilst simultaneously eating more pork scratchings than I've seen anyone consume before or since. It was an introduction to a quite extraordinary person that I wouldn't forget in a hurry. (Indeed the mere fact of my writing about it now, some ten years later, is testament to that.)

On the pitch Canton rewrote the rulebook, literally. No one from either team or any of the officials was allowed within ten yards of him, every time he had the ball we all had to applaud and cheer loudly and he was allowed to kick, punch or stab anyone he wanted to. No one else would have got away with it, but that was Canton all over:

the sort of person who could get away with things that no one else could.

Personally I had quite a good relationship with Canton, and the other older lads for that matter. They kind of took me under their collective wings and formed a protective barrier around me, so much so that some games I wouldn't touch the ball or get anywhere near the action. At the time it seemed strange, but now I can see how beneficial it was to my game. So many youngsters think they know it all, reckon they can run before they can walk, and then get burnt out and find themselves on the scrapheap by the time they're twenty-one, their potential having dissolved like soluble aspirin in water or salt in water, or indeed sugar. Not me. I was one of the lucky ones. Thanks to my more experienced team-mates I learnt to crawl first, then walk, then skip a little, then jog lightly and finally, when I was sure I'd mastered all those other steps, run.

The rest of that season was dominated by Canton. Football's a team game, but he was a one-man team, doing the job of eleven players and, sometimes, even the substitutes as well. When he was on song, we'd coast through matches, often losing by only one or two goals and sometimes even getting a draw. But when he was off song things wouldn't go so well. I remember one game Canton turned up wearing a full scale model of The Kremlin fashioned into an off-the-shoulder number. And another where he believed he was the reincarnation of Champion the Wonder Horse. Needless to say we didn't fare so well in either of those games, though we did save some children who had fallen down a disused mine shaft during the latter.

At the end of that season, though, we'd proved a lot of our critics wrong. Most people in the pub had been saying we'd never win anything and whilst they were right in terms of cups, league championships and the like, they were wrong when it came to sendings off. We topped the sendings off league by a mile – Canton alone could have done that – and so the last laugh was ours.

From my point of view that first season in the senior team had been a great success. I'd established myself as a regular in the side and was building up quite a reputation. In the pub and around the local area people would point me out. 'That's David Feckham,' they would say. Or, 'David Feckham that is.' I felt I'd easily done enough to win the player of the year award, but decided it wouldn't be fair on the other lads, who, despite their lack of ability, had all put in two hundred and ninety-one per cent. So I discreetly had a word with everyone and told them not to nominate me. It worked a treat and I got no votes at all, the award going to Miggsy.

But looking back on that year from where I am now, as opposed to from where I was last year or the year before, I can see that it marked something of a transition for me, not just in terms of my footballing development, but in terms of the bigger picture as well.

Before I knew it I was twenty and even though I still slept with a teddy bear, played with Lego and occasionally wet the bed, I was no longer a kid. It was time to strike out on my own.

Of course Uncle Cedric and Aunt Delia didn't want me to leave. Their own kids had been taken into care years ago, but after one night when Aunt Delia climbed into my bed and told me that a woman of her age still had needs, I knew it was time to go. (The stewed apples every morning, noon and night hadn't helped either.)

The bedsit I moved into was a home from home. It was part of an old and very large building – I had to share a kitchen and bathroom with 117 other people – and if anything my room was even smaller, damper and smellier than the one I'd had at Cedric and Delia's. But once I'd put my Manchester United posters up it took on a completely different quality, one that it retained even after the posters had disintegrated due to the damp, so I was well happy.

The best thing about it though was that Miggsy, Scooby, Brevilley and Puttsy also had their own places nearby. Three bus rides, a walk, another two bus rides and a short run through a particularly rough estate and I could be hanging out with the lads.

We were inseparable in those days and looking back we must have seemed just like any other bunch of lads – our personal hygiene was appalling, we masturbated furiously at every given opportunity and we drank dangerous amounts of alcohol and got into fights. But unlike other lads who had bought a one-way ticket on the fast train to nowhere, we had football. And football had us. Yes, it was a great time, but, incredibly, it was about to get even better.

I first clapped eyes on Vivian when her covers band Copycats came to play in The Schnitzel and Parrot. Well, clapped ears on her would be more accurate. I was cleaning Uncle Cedric up, after he'd messed himself, and all I can remember is hearing this beautiful, beautiful voice wafting through the toilet cubicle. It seemed to be singing to me and me alone.

'Hurry up 'Arry, cam on. We're going down the pub,' it was saying, in a credible impersonation of Sham 69's Jimmy Pursey.

'Sorry, Uncle Cedric,' I said letting him fall back down into his mess.

I ran out of the Gents my heart beating faster than a very anxious person on crack. Having clapped ears on her, I now clapped eyes on her, and then, because the song had finished, clapped hands. There were five girl singers and a motley backing band in the Copycats, but I was just focused on one person. She was the most beautiful creature I had ever seen. Clad from head to toe in a purple PVC jumpsuit and topped off with a plastic tiara in her hair she looked incredible. As she started singing the next song, 'Seven Tears' by The Goombay Dance Band, I floated on a cloud of pure love energy over to where the lads were sitting. Then, that cloud burst and my feelings rained out.

'Phwooooaaarggghhhhh!' I said to the lads, drenching them with passion. 'Who the fuck is that bird? She's fucking gorgeous.'

'That, mate, is Vivian, and you have two chances with her: none and fuck all,' said Puttsy.

'Yeah, well we'll see about that,' I said.

The lads looked at me. They knew that look in my eye only too well, it was the one that said, *I'm really, really deadly deadly serious*; at least it would have done if I hadn't had really bad conjunctivitis at the time. It was time to hatch a plan.

Since Donna I hadn't actually spoken to another girl. I'd tried to, but used to get hysterical blindness and would run away screaming and smash into anything higher than one metre. Or they would. This time was going to be different. With the plan hatched I started putting it into action.

I ran back into the bogs and hauled Uncle Cedric up.

'Come on, Uncle Cedric, I know you've helped me out loads already, but if you do this for me, I'll buy you a Porsche when I'm playing for Man United.'

And I was serious, deadly serious, as that look in my eye earlier would have told anyone who knew me had I not had conjunctivitis.

Uncle Cedric was heavier than I'd expected, but after some considerable effort I'd managed to get him out of the

Gents and into the Ladies, leaving only a small trail of shit along the way.

I stood outside the entrance to the Ladies. I knew she'd have to come in here eventually, it was just a matter of waiting.

Forty-five minutes later, after fending off thirty-seven other irate women and two trannys, Copycats closed their set with a version of 'Stations of the Crass' by Crass. As cheers and shouts of 'Get yet tits out for the lads' resounded around the pub I braced myself for action. As luck would have it, she was the first of the band to need a slash. I saw her approach the toilet and felt the nerves rise. A scream began to edge its way up my throat, presumably towards my mouth. I fought it and pushed it back down past my throat and into my lungs.

Then she was in front of me. Our eyes locked, hers deep blue, mine grey and bloodshot. It was now or never.

'I wouldn't go in there love,' I managed to blurt out.

'Why the fuck not, I'm bustin',' she said in a voice that melted my heart.

'Old geezer's fucking crashed out on the floor and shat himself,' I said. I could feel the scream rising and my legs setting themselves to run, but she was my damsel and she was in distress. I had to save her.

'You could always go in the Gents and I'll watch the door for you.'

She looked at me.

'Okay.'

Then.

'What's all that gunk in your eyes?'

'I got conjunctivitis ain't I?' I said.

'Right. Well make sure no fucker comes in, all right?'

I followed her to the Gents like a lap dog, my tongue hanging out of my mouth like a large sock.

She was in there for ages and I had to smack a couple of geezers who wanted to go in, and one of the trannys, but I protected her and for that she was grateful.

Half an hour later, after we'd had a knee-trembler round the back of the pub, I was totally smitten.

'Can I see you again?' I said.

'Yeah, all right,' she said.

From then on me and Vivian were an item. It wasn't easy at first though. She was very busy with Copycats and I had football – playing, training, watching it on telly, watching it on video, talking about it in the pub with me mates, playing it on video machines in arcades, playing it on my PlayStation, Subbuteo, and thinking about it – all of which meant we used to spend hours on the phone to each other. Sometimes we were happy saying nothing, happy just knowing each other was there, though on quite a few occasions I stayed on the phone for two hours without realising Vivian had actually hung up.

I also used to shower her with presents. Whichever pub she was playing in I'd ring up and get a packet of cheese and onion crisps, her favourite flavour, sent to her.

As for football, whenever she could, Vivian would come and watch me play. And every time she did it seemed to spur me on to play even better. Of course she didn't really understand the game. I spent hours trying to explain to her that the players wearing the same clothes as me were on my team and the players wearing different clothes were on the other team, but she never grasped it. She kept asking questions like 'What's the ball for?' and 'Are you allowed to hop?' On the whole though I think she enjoyed watching me play. That's the thing about being in love, you could watch the person you love doing anything – making custard, building a model of the Eiffel Tower out of matchsticks, or putting on a badge – and still be happy.

From the millisecond I first met Vivian I knew I wanted to spend my life with her, or marry her, whichever was the longer, but it wasn't until we'd been seeing each other for about six months that I actually asked the question.

I found a ring in an old Christmas cracker. It was red, Vivian's third-favourite colour, so I knew she'd like it. I wasn't one for going overboard so I just popped the question one night after I'd taken her out for a romantic meal – egg and chips down the local burger bar.

'Oi,' she said in that shrill, grating voice I knew and loved so well. 'Oo do you fink I am? Ask me proper or you can forget it mate.'

Just then a fight broke out in the burger bar because some kid had thrown up over another kid. With chairs flying overhead and the stench of vomit in the air, I got down on one knee.

'Vivian,' I said, 'I love you and want to spend the rest of my life with you. Will you—' And then my mind went completely blank. I don't know what it was – nerves, stress, anxiety, tension or maybe something else – but like an actor I just totally forgot my lines.

Looking up at Vivian I could see that she was losing interest. Her attention span wasn't great and if I didn't remember what I had to say soon, the moment would be gone, maybe for ever.

Luckily fate has a way of playing tricks on us and this was one of those times that the magician fate took to its stage and performed just such an act of legerdemain on my behalf. A chair hit me with its full force on the back of my head. It seemed to jolt me out of my mental impasse and, just before I blacked out, I shouted, '—marry me?'

I don't remember what happened next, but when I came

to Vivian was there and she was wearing the ring. Even though I hadn't heard it, she had said yes. I couldn't have been happier, unless I'd been picked to play for Manchester United.

The next step was to get the approval of Vivian's dad. I know in this day and age that might seem old-fashioned, but that was the kind of guy I was, and the kind of guy I still am, and the kind of guy I'm sure I still will be if you were to ask me in the future. So, the very next day we drove down to London.

Yes, London. Incredibly it turned out that Vivian had grown up near to where I had. Right next door to me in fact, but I'd just never spotted her.

I felt a surge of nostalgia surge through me as I turned into what had been my street. I think I was probably more nervous than that first time with Vivian down the lavs in the Schnitzel and Parrot, but at the same time I was also less nervous. As Vivian's dad opened the door I readied myself.

'This geezer wants to marry me. All right?' Vivian blurted out before I could say a word.

Vivian's dad, Mr Fox, took one look at me and then collapsed clutching his chest. Not having spoken to him for almost a year Vivian was unaware that he'd developed angina. Clearly the happiness and excitement had been too much for him and brought on a heart attack or perhaps a coronary. Luckily it turned out to be a minor one and he was only hospitalised for three months.

I was overjoyed at being accepted into Vivian's family and desperate to tell mine, but I still had no idea where they were. I did have Uncle Cedric and Aunt Delia though. They were delighted for me. Uncle Cedric celebrated by single-handedly drinking the pub dry and Delia celebrated by offering to be the stripper at my stag do. The lads were also made up. Yeah, they took the mick a little, going on about how me and Viv were like David Beckham and his bird, that Posh Spice, only much poorer, uglier and less talented, particularly in my case, but that's part of being one of the lads, isn't it, taking the piss? Underneath it all I could tell they were made up for me.

As the next season began I was on cloud nine. I'd trained especially hard over the summer and was raring to go. Our first match was away to The Hairy Plughole and was notable for a goal that people still talk about to this day. It was early in the second half and, with most of the action on the other side of the pitch, I was standing just inside our opponents' half chatting to Vivian who was on the touchline.

'Yes, you do need a ball, Viv,' I was saying, 'because something needs to go into the net so that we know when a goal has been scored.'

'What's a goal?' said Viv.

She was priceless and I was about to give up my explanations for another day when, as luck would have it, the ball landed by my feet. It was too good an opportunity to miss.

'This is,' I said and walloped the ball as hard as I could. It flew up in the air, higher and higher.

'Is that a goal yet?' said Vivian.

'No. Wait,' I said.

Still higher it went until, having reached its own particular zenith, it plummeted down to earth again, over the goalie's head and into the back of the net.

'That's a goal,' I said.

'Yeah,' said Brevilley, who was now standing beside me. 'An own goal.'

'Oh no,' I said holding my head in my hands. I was

devastated. Explaining a goal to Vivian was hard enough; explaining an own goal would be nigh on impossible.

CHAPTER 6:

Proud, Prouder, More Prouder

'A flight of stairs and a medallion of beef.'

Do you know how many people play Pub Sunday League football? No, nor do I, but in a pure maths sense, it's loads. There are teams all over the country, in cities, towns, villages – even in Hamlets. And in the hurly burly of their weekly matches, every Pub Sunday League player is passionate about their team. It makes complete sense. Players see each other week in week out. They eat fish together. They go to fêtes together.

But, whenever the *national* Pub Sunday League team is mentioned, you can see a change on players' faces. However dedicated they are to their local side, most will drop that team like a slow-burning piece of coalite, just to get a sniff of the national side.

Over the years, I'd spent hours fantasising about playing for the national team. In one of my dreams I'd be saving a near-certain goal, then dribbling the length of the pitch and scoring one. In another, I'd be scoring with a bicycle kick as I dismounted a penny-farthing. And in a third I'd be slow-dancing on the pitch with the entire cast of *Coronation Street* and several of the programme's sponsors.

The national manager, Jem Soddle, was known to pick his favourites – the sort of players who sent him selections of pre-wrapped buffet finger foods or spun gold thread for him on ancient looms.

But even though he'd received nothing from me, I felt pretty certain that I was in with a shout.

So when I first opened the letter, I have to say I wasn't surprised.

Pub Sunday League World Cup Finals – France 1998
Player Selected: David Feckham

I immediately phoned the Pub Sunday League HQ and got through to Soddle's PA, Angela Bartlett.

'I was expecting your call,' she said. 'You want to know what you're doing in the national team?'

'I expected it,' I replied. 'I'm twenty-three. My time has come. I just want to know when he scouted me, where he wants me to play and if I'm going to be captain.'

Angela was very diplomatic.

'It's complicated,' she told me.

I roared with laughter, warming immediately to her dry sense of humour and acerbic comic timing.

She hadn't finished her mirth-soaked yarn.

'Soddle picked his favourite twenty-six players but couldn't decide on the twenty-seventh. To help him focus his mind, he decided to play eighteen holes of golf. This would have been a great strategy but he insisted on playing them in the kitchenette of the Pub Sunday League Association's headquarters. Instead of telling him not to be so stupid, his minions colluded with his wishes a) by filling the kitchenette with lush turf and sandy bunkers and b) by dressing up as caddies.'

'Incredible!' I mused.

'After an hour without him saying anything, his staff were getting frustrated but he was on a birdie at the ninth and was totally focused.'

'The man's a legend,' I whispered.

'Anyway,' said Angela, 'in the end, he told his assistant Roger Turnbull to open the file on his laptop containing the name of every single Pub Sunday League player in England and to scroll down the humungous list. When Soddle shouted "Stop!" he told Turnbull to hold the mouse.'

'Awesome,' I murmured.

'Your name was highlighted. That's how you got the gig.'

I loved Soddle's acting skills. To pretend I was a random selection would give hope to the thousands of youngsters who believed they had a future in football.

'Brilliant,' I told Angela.

'The squad are going to La Twanga in Spain to warm up. While there, Soddle will whittle down the twenty-seven to twenty-two. That means five players will be devastated and possibly destroy their rooms.'

'Heavy duty,' I muttered.

'I'll bet my life and the lives of my entire family that you'll be one of those five,' Angela explained.

I chortled with delight. Angela was something else.

'Would you like to go out some time, as a friend, for a drink?' I asked cheekily, 'or perhaps even a beverage?'

'In your dreams, little man,' she responded before hanging up.

I phoned the lads straight away and to my delight discovered they'd all got the call.

'It's going to be unreal!' I told them. 'Us in France, surrounded by the world's greatest players.'

'And croissants,' added Brevilley.

Meeting up with the squad was an incredible experience. Scooby sat on a luggage trolley and I pushed him around the departure lounge at Heathrow until a stern security officer waved an Uzi sub-machine gun in our faces and told us to stop.

I was there not just with my mates, but with some of the most legendary names in Pub Sunday League football. My all-time hero, Stazza, was juggling with a bunch of Italian kids, whose parents were whooping with joy. I'd watched him as a lad and admired his clinical skills.

The flight out to Spain was a brilliant laugh. Me and Scooby nicked all of the complimentary sour cream and onion pretzels and wolfed them down in one of the toilets. We were giggling crazily at the time but weren't so happy fifteen minutes later when we both got the worst heartburn either of us had ever experienced. (And of course we couldn't take anything for it because all chewable over-the-counter heartburn remedies contain the performance-enhancing steroid Grandmadrilone.)

Walking into the resort was fantastic. The England national team were staying there as well. But we weren't allowed any contact with them.

Soddle was very keen on us training all day and playing practice matches. He worked out a full schedule for us, but left it to the coaches while he went off to play golf. He just didn't want to be anywhere near us. The golf course out there was beautiful and he had a great new set of clubs. And who could blame him? The guy lived football in the rest of his life, why not make the most of the facilities.

I do, however, have to criticise him for the way he culled the squad from 27 to 22. There had been lots of rumours, some involving circus animals, but none of us knew how he was thinking.

One afternoon after training he put up a notice. It listed a thirty-second appointment for each of us. I was twenty-seventh. I couldn't tell if this was good, bad or somewhere in between.

After the first few appointments, it became clear that this system was ludicrous. We were sitting on the floor outside his room and lads were just going in and out when called. Soddle had placed two cards on the wall which read YES and NO. When you walked in, he pointed at one of them with a snooker cue. That was it. No explanations. No supportive chats.

When Brevilley walked out of his meeting with Soddle, I knew straight away that he was upset about something.

'Was it the room service?' I asked.

He shook his head and I saw the water filling his eyes.

'I didn't make the cut,' he explained, 'I need some time alone.'

And the same happened with Stazza. I couldn't believe it.

'I'm not in the frame,' he said quietly.

I didn't know what to say, so I said, 'Is that good or bad?'

He scowled and walked off to his room. He was totally choked and some of the lads said he rearranged his room according to the principles of feng-shui. Earlier that day, Stazza had told me: 'I love you David. You shouldn't be here, but you are. And that's good. I don't think you'll make it into the twenty-two, but I reckon you have a pretty good future, possibly in insurance.'

Scooby was twenty-sixth and he gave me a thumbs-up when he came out.

I took a deep breath and walked inside.

Soddle was practising knocking golf balls into a paper cup with his snooker cue.

'David,' he said as I walked in. He then pointed at the word YES with the cue. 'I think it will be good fun to have you there. Give the troops something to laugh at.'

'Th . . . thanks, boss,' I stammered.

'Close the door on your way out,' he muttered.

81

And that was that. I was in the 22, but two of my best mates weren't.

I had to accept it. I had to go with it. I had to get some travellers' cheques.

Vivian was chuffed for me, when I phoned her. 'Will you be raking in loads of cash?' she asked.

'It's not about money, Vivian,' I explained. 'It's about pride and recognition.'

'Yeah I know, David, but will you be raking in loads of cash?'

After we returned from La Twanga, I totally dedicated myself to training, sometimes not stopping for a break for 72 hours.

When it came round to heading out for France, I felt fresh and prepared. Once again we were staying at the same hotel as the England team. Except this time, we were told it would be okay to mix with them, if we wanted.

For our first game against Tunisia I was on the bench. For the second game against Romania I was also on the bench. For the third game against Colombia I was on the bench too. On all of these occasions I wasn't a substitute. I was just sitting on a bench nowhere near the others.

We made it through the group stage and found ourselves up against Argentina. We had a bit of a history with the Argentinians. In the early nineties, their Pub Sunday League side were fond of red wine and our predecessors had publicly expressed their disgust at this haughty preference.

Once again, for the Argentina game I was on a bench. Incredibly Soddle ambled over. He was really tired from the night before and slept next to me for the entire first half. It was 2–2 at half-time and Soddle continued to sleep. So Roger Turnbull did the team talk. He said the lads were doing well but that the game at that stage was a draw. We needed to score again to win. Some of the boys nodded earnestly. These wise tactical comments were gems.

The lads came out for the second half and it became clear quite soon that we might need to shake things up. Turnbull indicated after ten minutes that he wanted to make a change. At that moment, Soddle turned in his sleep and brushed against me with his arm. Turnbull looked at me with amazement but, to his eyes, Soddle's instructions had been clear. I trotted over to Turnbull and before he could say anything I was on the pitch.

The grass was so freshly cut that for a few seconds I knelt down and licked it. The Argentinians must have known what sort of package I was, because after thirty seconds I'd been unpacked. Our captain and centre forward, big Anton Clearer, hoofed the ball in my direction. Flimeone, their legendary defender, floored me as I was about to sneak past him. As he towered over me, he whispered in my ear, 'You're it.' I understood at once what he was up to. Playing a concurrent game of 'tag' was a stroke of inspiration and I knew what I had to do. I raised my foot a bit and flicked him ever so gently. That way I'd tagged him and he might not even know about it.

But the ref wasn't having it. He reached into his pocket and pulled out a red card.

'You're joking aren't you?' I shouted. 'He's it!'

'Why do you imperialist bastards expect the whole world to speak your language?' he responded in perfect Estuary English.

I started to walk off in disbelief. Soddle was still asleep. I looked back at the ref, but the game had started again. I went straight into the tunnel and headed for an early bath.

We lost the game 3–2 and afterwards the lads walked into the changing room looking bitter and dejected. No one spoke to me, apart from Toby Edams.

'Look, David,' he began. 'You've just fucked up most of our lives, but that's not the main point here.'

'What is the main point?' I asked.

'Are we products of societal fragmentation or are we free beings?'

I'd heard he'd recently got into philosophy.

'Are you asking from a Foucaultian perspective or as a third-wave Marxist?' I enquired.

'Shut up you snivelling little git,' he replied.

I could see both of his points of view.

We travelled back to our base at La Baule. I would have turned in for an early night, but found myself in the games room, playing darts and Rummicub with some of the lads. No one said anything. I didn't know if that was because of the emotions we were feeling or because of the sign saying NO TALKING above the door.

At about four a.m. I went upstairs and was just turning the key to my room, when I felt a tap on the shoulder.

'Fucking hell!' I exclaimed. 'David Beckham.'

He smiled.

'If it isn't David Feckham.'

I suddenly remembered that the official England team had played as well that night, also against Argentina.

'How did you lot get on?' I asked.

He looked at the floor for a few seconds. 'It was a nightmare. We lost 3–2 and I got sent off. I hardly touched the guy.'

'No way!' I responded. 'That's exactly what happened to us. I was sent off too. For nothing.'

Beckham shook his head. 'I wonder how people are going to take it?'

'I think they'll still respect me,' I answered.

'No, mate, I mean about me.'

I put my arm round his shoulders.

'Don't worry mate, your profile's not that high.'

He looked at me quizzically. 'Don't you read the tabloids?' he asked.

'I've always preferred a broadsheet.'

'Well, David, I hope next time we meet we'll both have some good news.'

'Totally,' I grinned, 'and don't worry. No one will take any notice of what happened to you tonight. It won't make any of the papers.'

He looked at me with warmth.

'Cheers, mate,' he said, 'that's made me feel a bit better.'

'No worries,' I smiled.

He walked down the corridor and disappeared round a corner.

I let myself into my room and flicked on the TV. The sound was down and I just watched a couple of pundits sitting in front of a huge image of a Beckham lookalike, shouting and gesticulating wildly. I turned it off and lay down on my bed.

The next thing I knew it was morning and there was a long scroll of paper lying on my chest. I unfurled it and stared at the fax print.

It was the front page of the *South Manchester Argus*. 'Local boy a hero for kicking Argentine bully.'

I sat up and studied it more carefully. The article was about me. I couldn't believe it. They were hailing me as a national superstar because I'd flicked Flimeone. It even said in the article that I should be up for a knighthood, Victoria Cross or shares in Port Stanley Airport.

I sat by the phone waiting for the calls from the national press. Then I checked my watch and realised we were an hour ahead of them, so it would only be ten a.m. in Blighty. Most of those journalist types were probably still asleep in their loft apartments in the square mile or preparing dinner parties for politicians at which they only eat rocket and then pretend to be sated.

Suddenly the phone rang. I leapt to answer it.

'David Feckham,' I answered quickly.

It was Vivian.

'David, you need to come home now,' she insisted.

'Why?' I asked.

'The Copycats have split up and it's getting nasty.'

I furrowed my brow.

'What sort of nasty?' I enquired.

'Our bass player Chester has locked himself in his guitar case and is refusing to come out until we make him a full round of club sandwiches and start calling him Cordelia.'

I was ready with a diplomatic answer.

'How about forcing the catch and dragging the bastard out?' I suggested.

'Excellent idea, David.'

I listened carefully as I heard her shouting in the background.

'How about forcing the catch and dragging the bastard out?'

This was followed by cheers and riotous noises.

A few seconds later Vivian was back on the line.

'He's out,' she said with relief. 'He's dropped the club sandwiches bit, but is sticking to the Cordelia request.'

'Talk him down to Cord,' I said with authority.

She went away again, only to return moments later.

'We've agreed on Cordel,' she informed me, 'but the Copycats are history.'

'Maybe I can help the band re-form?' I offered.

'Forget it! I don't ever want to have anything to do with those talentless airheads. Now get your arse back to the UK,' she commanded.

I was desperate to talk about last night's match and the

piece in the *South Manchester Argus*, but I could hear in her voice that she was too preoccupied for such matters.

'I'll be on the next plane home,' I told her.

'You better be,' she said.

The airport was pretty deserted as was the plane. I was the only passenger and the cabin crew did an extended version of the passenger instructions. I particularly liked the section about using a life raft, but they really didn't need to inflate it in the aisle. Two of them were crushed and a third had to pierce the body of the raft with an earring.

Vivian was waiting at Heathrow.

'What are you doing here?' she asked me as I approached her.

'I've just got back from France to meet you. What are you doing here?'

'I'm waiting for my brother Angus. He's coming back from Las Vegas and took a bit of a financial hammering.'

'Is there room in the car for me?' I asked.

She looked doubtful, but I pleaded and she relented.

In the end, we left without Angus.

Apparently he had to wait two hours for a train and got stranded in St Albans.

Vivian was clearly distraught about the break-up of the Copycats.

'They were all crap musicians,' she told me, 'but I needed them to get my face known. It's better to have live musicians than poorly produced karaoke backing tapes.'

I reminded myself to hide away the collection of poorly produced karaoke backing tapes on my bedroom shelf.

'So what's next, babes?' I asked her. 'Do you get a new band or what?'

'I don't know, David. There are a lot of musicians who want to play with me, but I need to choose the right ones.

Anyone who wants their face in the spotlight alongside my visage can go fuck themselves.'

I squeezed her arm. That was one of the things I liked best about her. She was feisty, spirited and very career-orientated. I made a mental note to urge her one day in the future to write a self-help book about crushing people who stand between you and your stated goal.

In spite of her upset about Copycats, as soon as we left the airport we at once felt again the electrical force that surrounded us whenever we were together.

'Let's put the Copycats behind us for the night,' Vivian said. 'Let's just large it together.'

I knew it was going to be a night of romance. First we took in a quality meal at a gastro pub, close to her parents' house. I was so nervous I only managed the gargantuan double roast dinner. Vivian went for the braised chicken salad and a side of gobstoppers. Everything was right in the restaurant. The lighting was dim, the food was excellent and the pianist went through the entire Motorhead back catalogue.

Vivian wiped her lips delicately after enjoying a frothy cappuccino. I took my time with a latte.

'Back to mine?' she asked seductively.

'What about your mum and dad? You know I hate it when they listen at the door and laugh,' I said.

'Don't worry,' she reassured me. 'They're out at a charity auction for neglected hedgerows.' (Vivian's mum and dad are very keen gardeners.)

Half an hour later we walked into her parents' place.

We didn't waste a second.

I chilled the bitter lemon.

She warmed the breadsticks.

'Let's do it,' Vivian commanded coquettishly, disappearing off to her room.

As we fell on the bed together, I blessed the Mates machine in the gents' toilet at Heathrow. My eleven condoms fitted perfectly. They formed an unenviable love block.

'Come on baby,' purred Vivian.

I can honestly say that it was the best night of love-making I'd ever experienced. Immediately afterwards, Vivian pulled out her judging cards and held up 9.7.

'What about the other 0.3?' I enquired.

'That's for the split condoms.'

'What are you on about?'

I looked down and was stupefied by what I saw. In a probability stakes of one in ten trillion, each of the eleven condoms had burst in exactly the same place.

'Oh my God,' I cried.

'Don't worry, babes,' said Vivian. 'Whatever happens, it will be okay.'

And four weeks later, I discovered that 'whatever' had happened.

'We're going to have a child,' Vivian told me on the phone.

I gasped. 'What sort of child?' I asked.

'A CHILD, DAVID,' she yelled. 'A KID. A BABY. A LITTLE ONE. A NIPPER. A BAIRN.'

'All right, all right,' I responded, 'I just wanted to be clear.'

I popped over to her parents' house later that evening.

'You dirty little bastard,' screamed her dad.

I leapt backwards, defending my crotch and face at the same time.

But he just started laughing. 'I'm only joking, son,' he beamed. 'We're delighted. We can think of thousands of blokes who'd make a better father for our first grandchild, but we accept that you have to roll with the hand life deals you. So welcome to the family, David.'

It suddenly made me realise how much I missed Mum and Dad and my sisters.

I knew, though, that I could do more to ingratiate myself with Vivian's parents. Sure, I was siring grandkid number one, but I had much more to offer them.

So, after doing an evening class at the local adult education centre, as a surprise I fashioned some ornate topiary designs in their front garden.

It was clear that Vivian's dad was particularly chuffed.

'A flight of stairs and a medallion of beef,' he noted as he took in my garden art.

Vivian's mum burst out crying and ran inside the house. I loved her for this. She wasn't content just to be a silent patron of the arts. The whole *process* really moved her.

There was one downside to my hedge-cutting exercise. Apparently, I'd contravened local planning laws by making their garden fascia a couple of centimetres lower than the other properties in their street. For this, they were ordered to pay a hefty fine or spend six months with a team of German TV presenters in the New Forest, armed only with a tin of Alphabetti Spaghetti and two hammocks. They chose the former.

Vivian's pregnancy was an incredibly exciting time. The pub senior side were having a purple patch and Sralex Ferfuson was warming to me. I got a couple of runouts and he also made it very clear that he liked the sandwiches I made for the post-match debriefing sessions. I'd started off by just making a round for myself, but soon lots of the other lads indicated that they'd be grateful to have some for themselves. And then Sralex let me know that if I prepared some for him, my chances of playing would be greatly increased. As I lived next to a bakery, procuring bread wasn't a problem. Everyone presumed I worked there, as I was always wandering through the warehouse carrying a crate of loaves.

I mixed it up to make my offerings as varied as possible. Amongst the premium loaves I used were granary, rye and ciabatta.

'That's a bloody good BLT, David,' Sralex said one day. 'Have you ever thought of going to catering college?'

I laughed. 'Nice one, boss.'

His face remained uncreased by laughter lines. 'I'm totally serious, David.'

I walked off chuckling, and headed off to make sure my pear crumble hadn't congealed.

And amongst all of this football, there were the check-ups at the hospital, when I had a bad knee. A couple of times I bumped into Vivian there.

'Where have you been?' she shouted at me.

I pointed to the physio department.

'Have you forgotten, David? We're having a baby!'

The weird thing was, I had forgotten. Maybe forgotten is too harsh a word. It had slipped my mind. It's like when you're at the supermarket and, for the life of you, you can't remember the tuna chunks in brine.

Six months into the pregnancy, Vivian suggested we go to pre-birth classes.

I agreed to attend a) to show my commitment to our child and b) because there were only repeats on telly most Monday nights.

There were about fifteen couples at the class. It was okay there. A woman called Jenny told us what to expect in the birth and made us each swivel a model pelvis. One guy got a bit over-excited and Jenny had to snatch the thing back from him.

I sat next to a lad called Gary. He was a big Man United fan and we spent most of the class drawing up our fantasy United team of all time. After a few goes, he turned to me and whispered, 'Why do you keep writing Feckham instead of Beckham?'

I winked at him and carried on pretending to listen to Jenny.

Before we knew it, it was Vivian's due date. She'd wanted a home birth but her parents' stereo was twenty years old and she wanted to listen to some high-quality cover versions of great songs. So we went for the hospital option. They had two rooms with pools and I decided to take trunks and goggles for the day itself.

When we went on a tour of the hospital, I could hardly cover my disappointment.

'Our local pool's at least twenty-five metres and it's got a lido,' I hissed at one of the nurses.

She clipped me round the ear. 'If you'd gone private you'd have got the Olympic-size birthing pool.'

It happened in the middle of the night. I suddenly heard a gush of water emanating from Vivian's personage. In two seconds, the sheets were soaked.

'What do you think you're playing at?' I yelled as I woke up.

'My waters have broken, David.'

This was my moment. I leapt out of bed and did the following three things in this order.

1. Drank a litre of Appletise.
2. Played two rounds of *Gran Turismo* on my PlayStation.
3. Phoned the hospital.

Vivian was screaming in the bedroom.

I was tempted to ask her to tone it down, some of the other 117 residents were violent psychopaths, but by the time I spoke to a midwife I realised that I needed to get Vivian to hospital.

For some reason, I didn't take the car that night. Instead I used Maurice's motorbike. Maurice was a lovely bloke who lived in the next bedsit. I rode on the main part of the bike, while Vivian travelled in the sidecar. We made it to the hospital in record time.

A midwife was standing outside the hospital.

'Thanks for meeting us,' I said.

'I'm not meeting anyone. I'm just having a fag,' she replied.

Vivian was in a lot of pain by now and I carried her in a fireman's lift up the stairs. The lifts were playing silly buggers that night. As they stopped at each floor, the doors remained closed while a metallic voice offered you a modern European meal.

At last I reached the double doors of the maternity ward and strode in.

A midwife looked up from the station. It was the same one from downstairs.

'Thanks for meeting us,' I said.

'I'm not meeting anyone. I'm just having a bar of chocolate,' she replied.

Finally I found a midwife who looked like she was working the shift.

She took us straight to a labour room, and hooked Vivian up to the mains, or whatever they do. The pumping of our child's heartbeat sounded out. It was about 100 beats per minute and I wished that my old school-mate Deggsy (who's now a DJ) had been there to mix in some kicking sounds.

The midwife grinned at us.

'My name's Rachel, but you're to call me Genevieve.'

I nodded. Vivian screamed.

Genevieve did a quick inspection of Vivian and her face lit up.

'You're nearly fully dilated, love. You'll have a baby within a couple of hours.'

Ten minutes later, Genevieve suddenly shouted 'Push.'

I didn't realise she was talking to Vivian, so I started pushing the bed around the room as fast as I could.

'Stop it, you idiot,' Genevieve screamed.

As soon as I applied the brake, Vivian gave one enormous push and this tiny creature shot out. Genevieve had spent several summers being a wicket-keeper in a women's cricket team and was used to such deliveries.

'Is it a boy or a girl?' I shouted.

'Look at its dick,' Genevieve yelled.

'I know. But is it a boy or a girl?'

Vivian was sobbing her heart out. 'It's a boy, David. We've got a beautiful son.'

Genevieve was weeping as well and they both set me off.

Within seconds, I was gushing tears.

Genevieve let me cut the cord.

Vivian and myself held him together for the first time.

Vivian got out one of her breasts.

'Surely not now,' I said with horror.

Vivian looked to the heavens and attached the infant to her bosom. He started glugging with an intoxicated smile.

I gave Genevieve (who hadn't got a breast out) a side hug and walked over to Vivian and my new son.

It was the most incredible feeling in the world.

I was a dad.

It was like being a father.

But better.

CHAPTER 7:

The Treble (and my, David Feckham's, central role in securing it)

'Shit, next you'll be telling me it should be
Stone Sans ITC TT Bold'

There comes a time in one's life when you realise that some things are more important than football. Or so I'm told. Personally I haven't reached that point yet. I mean my dad never let having kids stand in the way of football, so I certainly wasn't about to. But don't get me wrong; having a son was still a big deal, that's why I had a tattoo done, to show how much it meant to me.

We'd always said we would call the boy after the place where he was conceived, but after much thought, decided that Viv's Room At Her Parents' House In Essex wasn't quite right. Instead we went for the place where I'd thought about the act of his conception on many a lonely night: my bedsit in Chorlton-Cum-Hardy. Then, after a minor fracas involving a jar of horseradish sauce (hot) at the office of registration of births and marriages, we were convinced to drop 'My Bedsit In'. So, Chorlton-Cum-Hardy it was (and still is to this very day).

As for the tattoo, there was never any doubt as to *where* I was going to put it, just above my arse; but the font, now that was a different story.

You look at any computer these days and the choice of

font is insane, it's incredible that clerical workers ever get anything done. Personally I've never been that adventurous, Times New Roman, Helvetica, Arial, if I want to make a good impression. But Vivian, she's a different kettle of fish. I guess it comes from being in the music biz, having that wild streak, but when she first suggested Copperplate Gothic Bold, I couldn't believe it.

'Blimey, Viv,' (my nickname for Vivian) I said, 'you can't be serious.'

'Yeah course I am. Though hang on a minute, maybe Optima Extrablack would be better. Or even Baskerville Semibold.'

'Shit, next you'll be telling me it should be Stone Sans ITC TT Bold,' I said, confident that that would knock her off her perch.

We loved arguing, me and Viv, did it all the time, still do in fact. It kind of makes us feel closer to each other, whilst at the same time, more distant.

'Yeah, that's it, Stone Sans ITC TT Bold, defo,' she said, taking my attempt to knock her off her perch and using it to knock me off my perch.

I knew that was it. End of argument, game over, checkmate. When Viv says defo, she means defo.

So that was that. Geezer in the tattoo parlour couldn't believe it when I told him, reckoned I was some kind of nutter, or a vegan. But even he had to admit it looked great when it was finished. Chorlton-Cum-Hardy in big Stone Sans ITC TT Bold letters stretching from just above the top left-hand corner of my left arse cheek, right across to just above the top right-hand corner of my right arse cheek.

When I got home I showed it to Chorlton-Cum-Hardy. As far as he was concerned it could have said 'Didsbury' or 'Rusholme', because he couldn't read yet, but somehow he seemed to know what it was. He gazed at it, then rubbed his hands all over the lettering. Unfortunately, because the font that I'd requested needed so much ink, it wasn't dry yet, and some of the lettering came off. All of 'Chorlton', and the final 'y' to be exact, leaving, well, you can work out what it left. It didn't bother me though. Well, you've got to laugh about these things don't you, otherwise you cry and cry and cry until you've no more tears left and all you can do is inhale huge great gulps of air as despair pierces every part of your being like bullets from a machine gun. So laugh we did.

I was still laughing about it as I pulled on my shirt for our opening game that season. The other lads thought I was mad, sitting in the corner of the changing room gibbering away to myself, but when I showed them why I was laughing they all started laughing too. Before we knew what was happening we were all rolling about on the floor, howling and crying with laughter. It was all fantastically homoerotic.

'Oi,' said Mr Ferfuson when he came in, which was all it took for us to stop rolling around laughing and sit up on the cold stone benches in abject terror.

'That's better,' he said. 'Now then, after certain events this summer, some of you might think that they're a bit special. They might think that they're something of a celebrity. They might . . .' He swung round and bored his eyes deep into my skull – it was ridiculously overdramatic, but then he wasn't an actor, so I could forgive him his thespian foibles. '. . . even think that they're a bit too good for this team. But let me tell anyone who *might* be thinking that . . .' He was standing right in front of me. I felt certain he'd had a lamb Korma the night before. He filled his lungs to bursting point. 'You're wrooooooonnnnnnggggggggg!'

He'd made his point and made it well. I wasn't entirely sure to whom in particular he was referring, Puttsy perhaps, but it certainly fired us all up for the match we were about to play.

Oh hold up, it was me! Mr Ferfuson was talking to me! Now I see it. Five years too bleeding late of course, but better late than never I suppose.

Anyway, now that I was an international, the weight of expectation nestled even more heavily on my shoulders, and the rest of my body, except my private parts. As we kicked off the new season I really felt that weight. My feet seemed to be sinking into the pitch. It wasn't until half time that I realised my feet actually had sunk into the pitch. Due to some unseasonably heavy showers, the ground was quite muddy, and what with my long studs, and the fact that I now weighed nearly eighteen stone, I'd become embedded into the turf. It wasn't a huge problem though. Not being able to move only hindered my game a little and all things considered I reckoned I'd had a decent enough first half. In fact I remained in that position throughout the half-time break and for the remainder of the game, narrowly missing out on the man of the match award.

Looking ahead I reckoned we were in for a long hard season. And as summer turned into autumn and then autumn turned into spring and then spring turned into summer and then summer turned into autumn again I was proved right. Every game was like a cup final. We were the team every other team wanted to beat, and generally did.

At home in the bedsit, now more of a bedstand since Chorlton-Cum-Hardy's arrival, Viv was juggling the demands of her career and motherhood. Her parents were especially good in that regard. Knowing how small our place was they never came to visit, except once when they were heading to a cottage in the Lake District for a short break and popped in to ask for directions. Uncle Cedric and Aunt Delia were also great, offering to look after Chorlton-

Cum-Hardy whenever we needed them to, an offer I'm sure we would have taken up had their place not been condemned as 'unfit for human habitation' by the Environmental Health Department.

By the time Christmas came around we were ninth in the table and sitting pretty, easily heading for mid-table respectability; a prospect made more appealing by the introduction of the Mid-Table Respectability Cup. This was a new initiative of FIFA's that they were piloting in our league. Basically it amounted to this: every year, there are usually five teams who, come February time, are in no danger of relegation or promotion, essentially teams with nothing to play for. Well, now they had something to play for. At the end of the season, those five teams would form a mini-league and play each other, with the team finishing in third place, i.e. in the middle of that table, being crowned winners of the MTR Cup.

It meant things became a little tricky for us. Of course we wanted to win games, but not too many in case we became a team who had something to play for and would thus be ineligible for the MTR Cup.

As luck would have it, though, we needn't have worried. We didn't win another game that season and ended up having a dalliance with relegation that turned into a full-on relationship, ending unpleasantly when we went our separate ways in an acrimonious split.

We survived that season thanks to an extraordinary final match against Die Doggen Und Ducken, a pub themed along the lines of a German beer cellar. They took the lead early on and hung on until the dying minutes. It looked like curtains for us, though as things turned out, it was more like drapes or perhaps blinds.

I picked up the ball in the middle of their half. I know I shouldn't have done – you're not allowed to use your hands in football – but there are an awful lot of rules, and sometimes it's hard to remember them all.

Being a team from a German theme pub, they were very organised and moved forward for the free kick in military fashion. As the ball was floated into our box I felt certain that one of their forwards would volley it into our net. But I hadn't counted on that British determination, the spirit of the Blitz, or is it Blintze? In an inspired managerial move, Mr Ferfuson put a CD containing the theme from *Dambusters* on his car stereo and turned it up to full volume. Instantly we were transformed. Scooby won the ball and, using his bare hands, started tunnelling down, down, down into our penalty area. The German theme pub team were nonplussed as they ran, like headless chickens, all over the pitch trying to figure out where he would come out. Twenty seconds later Scooby emerged, on their six-yard line. He squared the ball to Freddy Sheriff of Nottingham, who shot in to the top right-hand corner of the net. One each.

We were ecstatic. As a team we performed a conga around the pitch, followed by a hokey-cokey, and then paired up for a waltz. The German theme pub team were devastated. They were broken men, alive, but only in name only. Thirty seconds later Miggsy dribbled through them as if they were zombies before passing to our supersub, La Di Dar Gunner Solskbeer, who slotted home from close home on the range. Two–one.

Back in The Schnitzel and Parrot it was like a post-war street party only indoors. Bunting was everywhere and men were kissing women who they didn't know very well.

'Derek,' said Uncle Cedric.

'David,' I corrected.

'Yeah, whatever. You did good out there. You know what I'm going to do for you?'

'No,' I said, because I genuinely didn't.

'The treble,' he said with a seriousness in his eyes that I hadn't seen before.

I couldn't believe it. The treble was legendary in the pub. It was Uncle Cedric's special drink, a pint of rum, a pint of gin and a pint of cottage cheese. No one else had ever drunk it, and lived.

Uncle Cedric turned to face the bar. In fact he was facing the Gents, but when I turned him round again he was facing the bar.

'Spike,' he said. 'A treble, please.'

'Righto,' said Spike. Then, 'Gloria, be a love and do us a treble for Cedric.'

'It's not for me,' said Uncle Cedric.

Everyone stopped what they were doing. The whole pub came to a standstill and looked at me and Uncle Cedric.

'It's for Dere— David.'

Slowly the murmuring started. 'He'll never do it,' 'Twenty quid says he'll end up in hospital,' and, 'I've tried everything but I just can't get that axle-grease stain out of the carpet,' were just some of the things people were saying.

The treble arrived on the bar. I looked at Uncle Cedric. Uncle Cedric looked at me. I continued looking at Uncle Cedric. He continued looking at me.

'All right,' I said eventually, 'I'll pay for it.'

I handed over forty-five quid to Spike and lifted Cedric's personal tankard to my lips, because, in my book, that was the quickest route to my mouth.

I was just about to take my first sip when Vivian burst into the pub.

'No, David, no!' she screamed.

I looked at her. I knew she was thinking that now we had a kid I couldn't go around drinking lethal quantities of alcohol mixed with low-fat cheese.

'We can't afford it!'

But it was too late. Spike had pocketed the cash and was halfway to the bookies. I had no option but to drink. So drink I did. The whole lot.

It's hard to say exactly what happened next, but if anyone can tell me how, three days later, I found myself on the bus with the Manchester United players as they paraded the European Champions League trophy through town, I'd be very grateful.

My hangover lasted most of that summer, and I spent a decent proportion of it lying in a darkened room with an ice cube in my ear. But come August there was the small matter of a wedding to deal with. Mine. And Vivian's. Mine to Vivian is probably more accurate.

I left most of the preparations to Vivian. Well, I left all of the preparations to Vivian to be honest. She became a woman possessed. I remember she didn't take it too kindly when I suggested that maybe forty-seven bridesmaids, each dressed as one of her father's favourite Airfix models, was perhaps a little excessive. She wanted every little detail to be just right, even down to the special enamel paint on the Spitfire dress. Well, who can blame her? Every girl dreams of their wedding being the most fantastic day of their lives, don't they? When I saw how much it meant to her, when I saw her foaming at the mouth and pulling huge chunks of hair out as she screamed at the caterers, I knew that if anything went wrong, if the vol au vents weren't arranged on the plate in the shape of a mongoose, she well might sue for damages in the small claims court.

The only thing I did insist upon was the venue: on the pitch at Old Trafford. I knew you could get married there because I'd read about it in *Chat* magazine. Vivian didn't mind. It really was a beautiful pitch with plenty of room to erect a marquee.

Choosing my best man was something I wasn't really

looking forward to. Obviously it was going to be either Miggsy, Brevilley, Puttsy or Scooby, but which one? Night after night I would lie awake in bed weighing up their pros and cons. I hired a personal detective to compile a dossier on the four of them, but as luck would have it they each had exactly the same number of unsavoury habits. Finally, with my nails chewed down to the bone, both finger and toe nails, I decided there was only one thing for it: a Graeco-Roman-style wrestling match.

The following weekend, in a hastily constructed ring next to a layby on the M1, the contest took place. The lads stripped down to their underwear and, after covering themselves liberally in oil and balsamic vinegar salad dressing, got down to some serious grappling.

Half an hour later a victor emerged from the spider's web of limbs that lay in a heap in the middle of the ring: it was Brevilley. He was going to be my best man.

I was pleased at the outcome. Brevilley was a really funny bloke – I think he got it from his granddad who'd named his son, Brevilley's father, Breville Breville – and I knew he'd give a cracking speech.

The stag do was a relatively sedate affair. I was still hung over from the treble so Brevilley organised an evening of origami and ice-sculpture. It passed off peacefully enough, apart from a heated discussion as to how best to sculpt a young male falcon's talon.

I woke the next morning feeling refreshed and raring to go. Naturally enough I hadn't spent the night with Vivian in the bedsit, but the park bench I'd found was more than adequate, indeed marginally better than the bed we had. The arrangement was that Brevilley would pick me up at two-thirty, we'd meet the other guests at three, and then head down to the ground for three-thirty. The guests were mainly from Viv's side of the family. I still hadn't been able to contact my immediate family; I'd considered asking the private detective to trace them, but his fee, plus VAT and sandwich expenses, was just the wrong side of extortionate. As for Aunt Delia, she had a prior engagement shooting a Readers' Wives spread for *Fiesta* magazine, and Uncle Cedric said he'd love to be there, but felt it was more important that he went to the pub. He did wish me all the best though, which meant a lot. I'd also invited David Beckham, but apparently he had something on that day.

Everything went like clockwork to begin with. Brevilley was there at two-thirty, with the ring. We met the others and headed off to Old Trafford, arriving just before three-thirty. I was still feeling good. I mean it wasn't as if this was a big football match or anything, so what was there to get nervous about? I spotted Viv's mum and dad amongst the guests and waved to them. I think they waved back, though they may have mistaken me for a bookie doing tic tac toe and were in fact putting a tenner on Moscow Jet in the 4.00 at Aintree. That would explain why later in the day Mr Fox demanded his winnings from me.

Then, just after three-thirty I spotted Vivian. To say her entrance was amazing would be an understatement. Dressed from head to toe in white with a hint of lemon, she was wing-walking on a 1920s biplane flying overhead. And that wasn't all. The other four ex-singers of Copycats were on the other wing singing 'Video Killed The Radio Star' by Buggles, which was about as close to Biggles as she could get. (They'd agreed for this one-off reconciliation after extensive negotiations at ACAS.)

The plane landed and the pilot helped Viv down. She sashayed over to me.

'You ready then?' she said.

I didn't have to answer. The look on my face said it all. But I did anyway, just in case she couldn't read my facial expression so well.

'Yeah,' I said.

Arm in arm, with the Rabbi by our side – we hadn't been able to get a vicar – we marched towards the hallowed turf.

'Hello,' I said to the two burly security guards who stood by the towering entrance gates. 'We're here to get married on the pitch.'

They looked at each other. Then one of them, the burlier one, said, 'Not today you're not, son.'

I smiled. He was just doing his job, even if, in this instance, he was doing it badly.

'Yes it definitely is today,' I said, fixing him with my most earnest gaze. 'I wrote the date down on a yellow Post-it note which I have here in my pocket.'

I produced the note. I felt, in this psychological game of chess, it was a move that put me in an unassailable position. Surely the security guard had no option but to resign.

'Listen, son,' he said. 'I'm only going to say this once. You're not getting married on the pitch today because there's a game going on. United are playing Villa. Now, I could pop in there and ask everyone if they wouldn't mind taking a break for a while so that you can get married on the pitch, but, to use a somewhat well-worn and slightly trite expression, it's more than my job's worth. So, I'm going to count to five, and if you're still here I won't be able to vouch for the proximity of your head to your body. Is that clear?'

It was clear, crystal clear. That was why David Beckham hadn't been able to come to the wedding. He was playing. It all made sense. Then I remembered Viv. I looked at her and for a million-millionth of a second I thought that everything was going to be all right. Then the first punch caught me square on the nose and I knew I was wrong.

'I'll make it up to you, Viv, I'll make it up to you,' I shouted as the punches continued to rain down on me, and the kicks, stabs and Chinese burns.

'I've sorted it,' I said to Vivian three weeks later.

She looked at me. She hadn't stopped crying since that day outside Old Trafford and tears were still furrowing down her face and on to the floor. I really wanted her to stop, if for no other reason than she was ruining the carpet.

'Really,' I said taking her hand in mine.

'Really?' she said.

'Really,' I said.

'Really, really?' she said.

'Really, really,' I said.

'Really, really, really?' she said.

'Really, really, really,' I said.

'Really, really, really, really?' she said.

'Really, really, really, really,' I said.

It was the longest conversation we'd had in ages.

The following day me, Viv and Chorlton-Cum-Hardy met up with Brevilley and Viv's mum and dad and drove out into the countryside around Manchester. I've always loved the countryside; I sometimes wish the city could be more like the country, but then I guess it wouldn't be the city.

I parked the car by a church in a small village.

'Well, this doesn't seem too bad,' said Viv's dad.

'No,' agreed Viv's mum, who was a lot like Viv in many respects, only older and with a hairier moustache.

I smiled as I led my party towards the church and then past it.

'Wait a minute, Fecks,' shouted Brevilley. 'You've gone past it.'

'No, mate, you're the one that's past it.' I chuckled at my very, very clever joke. 'Come on, keep following me.'

They trudged on as I took them deeper, deeper and deeper still into the countryside. I could sense their nerves. Viv's dad in particular hated being away from pollution for too long and was getting quite edgy. Eventually I heard what I had been waiting for. It sounded like a sleeping dragon, but I knew it wasn't that, and not only because dragons don't really exist.

I led them over a final stile.

'Merci!' I said.

'Don't you mean, voilà?' said Viv's mum. She was right.

'Voilà!' I said.

And there it was for all to see. In the middle of a beautiful lush meadow stood an enormous hot-air balloon, ready to go. The vicar from that church and a pilot were waiting for us.

'Wow,' said Viv.

We all climbed aboard and as the balloon soared, so did my heart, though without the use of any hot air. It felt great being so high up and there and then I decided that it was much better than being low down.

We floated on for a little while and then the vicar gave a little cough which meant, 'I think it's time to start now.'

Me and Viv stood at one end of the balloon basket, with her parents to one side and Brevilley to the other. The vicar faced us whilst the pilot filmed it all on a video camera. It was brilliant. For about three minutes. Then we noticed that the wind was getting up a little. The first indication was Viv's dad beginning to feel queasy. The second indication was him being sick over Viv, and the third was the pilot screaming, 'Jesus, sorry vicar, there's a fucking hurricane brewing.' And he was right. Next thing we knew the balloon was being blown to kingdom come and we were hanging on for dear life. It was when a cow flew past me, followed by a Volvo Estate, that I knew we could be in for the ride of our lives.

Three thousand feet above the ground we thrashed around like the actors in *Star Trek* when the ship is under attack. Only this was for real. The pilot, Claude I think he was called, started desperately throwing anything he could get his hands on overboard. Out went the five-tiered wedding cake. Out went the three-tiered wedding cake. Out went the one-tiered wedding cake. And out, very nearly, went Chorlton-Cum-Hardy – he gained a reprieve when, after a secret ballot, we decided to offload a case of beer instead.

The women were screaming, the men were screaming, the vicar was screaming. I think we all thought it was the end. But I wasn't prepared for that. I looked from Viv to Brevilley to Viv's dad to the pilot to Viv's mum to the vicar to Chorlton-Cum-Hardy and then back to Viv again. 'Don't try and stop me,' I said. But, as I climbed on to the side of the heavily tilting basket, no one did.

I turned and, after taking one last look at Viv's mum, because her dress was riding up and you could see her knickers, I jumped. Straight into a freshly laid cow-pat. Now under normal circumstances I wouldn't have been happy about that, but this time I was over the moon.

'We're saved,' I shouted. And sure enough, once everyone had stopped screaming, they too could see that the balloon was in fact back on land.

Hugely relieved, everyone hugged each other, except me as I was covered in cow shit.

An hour later we were back in the local village pub and

having a laugh about it all. It turned out that we'd got caught up in Hurricane Nigel, a hurricane that was meant to have hit Jamaica, but had been blown off course by another hurricane, Trevor I think, and hit Manchester.

As for the wedding, the vicar conducted the ceremony in the field in which we'd landed. It was just like a normal wedding, except I had to stand thirty yards away from everyone else because of the stench, and so now me and Viv were husband and wife. She was Mrs Feckham.

It had all been quite an adventure, but the best thing about it was that the video camera had remained running throughout and the whole lot had been captured on film. We sent it in to a television programme called *Weddings That Went Horribly Wrong*, and the whole country got to see it. Overnight we became stars. Well, maybe not stars, but certainly on telly, and that was like being stars. And we got into the papers, which is also like being a star. Dross and Fecks they called us for some reason. But it was our moment, our fifteen minutes of fame, and with a bit of luck we hoped it might even last twenty minutes. Or even half an hour.

CHAPTER 8:

Me, Media Star, I (David Feckham)

'We just need the cumulative pot.'

I flicked the net curtain again. It was early on a Sunday morning and a bloke in a Ford Anglia was parked in the road directly outside the bedsit window, training a long lens on our window.

'I'm going out to talk to him,' said Vivian, getting out of bed and wrapping our fake Armani vole bedspread around her shoulders. I held Chorlton-Cum-Hardy and urged caution.

'Leave it, Viv,' I said, but only in my head, because if I'd said it out loud, I risked sending Vivian into one of her 'moods'. I watched out of the window as she strode across the road.

'What the fuck do you think you're doing?' she demanded as she reached the Ford Anglia.

The bloke looked shocked. 'Malcolm Gatley from the *Salacious Times*,' he said by way of an introduction. 'I'm just following instructions, love. I was told to get some pictures of you and David – you know, after the *Weddings That Went Horribly Wrong* thing. A lot of our readers want to follow the story.'

For a few seconds it looked as if Vivian was about to really lose it, but suddenly she started laughing.

'You wanker!' she yelled. 'We WANT the infamy and

notoriety. Come into the flat – you'll get much better shots.'

Malcolm looked bewildered. 'But I've only got the long lens,' he said.

'You can borrow my camera,' Vivian said, dragging him out of his car and towards the building.

Five minutes later, Malcolm Gatley was having a cup of tea in our bedsit and taking some photos of the two of us, with the 99p disposable camera Vivian had acquired at a hen weekend in Shepton Mallet. For the entire duration of the shoot, Vivian looked directly into the lens with an expression that mixed 'sultry' with 'phlegmatic'. I, on the other hand, kept pulling faces like 'Sardine' and 'The Orthodontist'.

And there was a lot of other media interest in us, the most exciting of which was a call from the *Robert and Julie* show.

We were nervous beforehand – their show was a national institution, and if we screwed up it could jeopardise both of our careers. But we needn't have worried. Their people did everything to make us feel comfortable, even calling us by our first names.

The producer was really friendly and sat down with us to go over what sort of things Robert and Julie might ask us. The questions she covered were all pretty standard apart from the geography multiple choice section.

Half an hour later, we were ushered down a whitewashed corridor and stepped out on to the stage beneath the glare of hot TV lights. There were several cries of recognition from the studio audience who were all sitting together in one very large chair.

Robert and Julie appeared a couple of minutes later and greeted us warmly. They introduced themselves, which wasn't really necessary. They were on TV every day and we knew who they were.

We exchanged some small talk, then some medium-sized talk, and before we knew it the floor manager was counting down. 'Five, four, three . . .' For some reason he mouthed the numbers '2' and '1' and I felt an urge to help him out. Maybe he was partially innumerate? But there was no time. The red lights flashed on the studio cameras. We were live.

Julie smiled at the camera. 'Good afternoon and welcome to the show,' she began. 'With us today we have the stars of *Weddings That Went Horribly Wrong* – the Feckhams.'

Then she turned to us. 'I must say, it's lovely to have you here. We followed your wedding day exploits along with the rest of the nation.'

'We did as well,' I replied.

Robert chipped in. 'Well, David and Vivian, your story has catapulted you into the public arena, hasn't it?'

'Our profile has definitely increased,' Vivian agreed.

'And how are you coping with this sudden fame?' asked Julie. 'I bet you're getting some interesting offers.'

'People have been great,' I nodded. 'I haven't been offered anything yet, but Vivian has been inundated by two things. The first was a radio ad for pretzels. We're still at the negotiating stage with that one.'

'Yeah,' nodded Vivian, 'but we turned down *Quality Lettuce Magazine* – their terms for the spread of me with a Romaine were unacceptable.'

'Are you thinking of chronicling your story in book form?' Robert enquired. 'It's just that we run a book club and an endorsement from us can ignite sales.'

'Of course,' nodded Vivian, 'we're in talks at the minute.'

This was news to me.

'How do you think everything will pan out?' asked

Robert. 'You know, when all of the initial fuss has died down?'

But we didn't get a chance to answer. The floor manager indicated an ad break and suddenly eight runners rushed over in our direction and picked us up on sedan chairs.

'Lovely to see you!' called Julie.

'Come back and tell us what happens,' smiled Robert.

The runners carried us away from the stage, raced down several dimly lit passages and threw us out of a side window.

'That was incredible,' I laughed, brushing myself down as Vivian climbed out of a skip.

We loved our time in the spotlight, but it wasn't all glitz, glamour and complimentary canapés.

One early evening we were returning home after a day out with Chorlton-Cum-Hardy at a Battle of Waterloo re-enactment, when we spied a very stern-looking policeman standing outside our block.

'What's happening?' Vivian asked.

'DI Robbins,' he informed us. 'Are you David and Vivian Feckham?'

We nodded, awed by his uniform and repulsed by his moustache.

'Look, there's no easy way of saying this,' he explained, 'but we picked up a gang in a dawn raid this morning. They have extensive contacts in the East London mafia.'

We looked at him in bewilderment.

'What's that got to do with us?' asked Vivian.

'Your fame has uncovered your whereabouts David,' DI Robbins explained. 'These people reckon you owe them, big time. They lost a lot of money on a massive football betting scam and they pin the blame squarely on your shoulders.'

I still didn't get what he was going on about. He leaned forward until his nose was jutting into my mouth.

'These people want to kidnap Ian,' he hissed, 'and they'll stop at nothing to get him.'

Vivian gasped. She loved that goldfish.

'Is that because they're really unlucky at funfairs?' I asked.

DI Robbins pulled his face away from mine and shook his head.

'No. If they get the fish, they'll ask you for a ransom to have him returned.'

'But we love Ian,' said Vivian, who was sobbing by now. 'They *can't* take him. He was the first present David ever got me.'

This wasn't strictly true because Ian was our *fourth* goldfish. I just hadn't been able to tell Vivian that the other three had gone up through the great, silver Koi Carp gates in the sky, and that I'd replaced each one when she was out.

DI Robbins continued: 'Ian's being kept in a safe tank for the time being and he's had his identity changed to an anemone. It's better off that way.'

'When can we have him back?' asked Vivian.

He shrugged his shoulders. 'Possibly later tonight but possibly never.'

That answer made a lot of sense to me.

'Thanks,' I said, attempting to shake his hand, but instead he insisted we play several rounds of Stone, Paper, Scissors. We got to 3–3 and were just about to ask Vivian to set a tiebreaker, when his mobile went.

'DI Robbins,' he answered. He listened to the caller and nodded thoughtfully for a few seconds.

'I don't give a shit that there's been a massive hold-up in a petrol station,' he barked. 'Or that it was led by hardened career criminals armed with AK-47s. I'm out in the field here doing some *real* police work.'

He tutted, flipped his phone shut and kissed us both paternally on the forehead. 'I'll be in touch,' he promised, before disappearing into the night shadows.

We felt unsettled and yet somehow calm at the same time. And anyway, I figured that if anything did happen to Ian, goldfish number 5 was only a Pet Universe store away.

The following morning at seven-thirty, there was a loud knock on our front door. Vivian jumped out of bed, hoping for an update on the Ian situation. But the look of horror on her face made me realise it was something quite different. There at the door were Mum, Dad, Clare, Katie and Uncle Terry.

Dad pulled me towards him and gave me the most enormous hug, whilst Mum quickly went through my pockets.

'Nothing,' she said, with disappointment.

'Mum, Dad, Clare, Katie, Uncle Terry, it's brilliant to see you!' I shouted joyously.

They hurried past me, and immediately began to turn the flat over.

'What's going on?' shouted Vivian.

'We have a real thing about termites,' my dad explained. 'We couldn't bear it if you and David were living in the shadow of these despicable creatures.'

Half an hour later, they were finished. Dad held up the shell of a burnt-out teacake and Katie clung to a pound coin she'd found under the floorboards.

They all sat down on the sofa.

I gave Mum a side hug. 'I knew we'd be reunited again.'

'Stick the kettle on, son,' Dad instructed me.

As I was pouring water into the kettle, Vivian sidled up

next to me by the kitchen sink. She didn't look best pleased.

'I cannot believe what's going on,' she hissed. 'They disgust me!'

'Me too,' I nodded enthusiastically. 'I hate those bloody termites. They're invasive and represent a real threat to modern standards of hygiene.'

'Not the termites, David!' She slapped her forehead in distress.

But I wasn't listening to her properly. I was handing the teas round, feeling on top of the world.

'You got a digestive?' asked Mum.

I shook my head.

'Don't worry, I've got my own,' she replied, pulling a huge packet out of her handbag and handing one each to Clare, Katie and Dad.

I put out my hand to receive one, but Mum slapped it with her handbag.

Uncle Terry reached into a holdall (the kind criminals use when carrying a gun for a bank raid) and pulled out an enormous roll of paper.

'Sign here, here and here,' he commanded me, indicating several blue crosses.

'What the hell is it?' asked Vivian.

'It's a pre-nuptial agreement,' explained Dad, 'all the big stars have them nowadays. It's all very standard stuff. It's been designed to protect your and David's best interests. Now you've both got a nice little media career going, none of us would like to see either of you get hurt.'

'Don't sign it, David,' Vivian implored me. 'We should get a lawyer or at least a paralegal to look over it.'

But Terry had placed a pen in my right hand, yanked my right arm towards the contract and guided my hand to sign in all of the right places.

'Okay,' said Clare, blowing the ink dry with a cordless hairdryer. 'This is the way it works.'

Katie picked up the baton. 'You've just agreed that Mum and Dad will be your managers, myself and Clare will be your PAs and Uncle Terry will be your PPM.'

'What's a PPM?' Vivian asked.

'Personal Protection Manager,' Uncle Terry replied, cracking his knuckles.

I was loving it. Not only had they tracked me down, but they actually wanted to be deeply involved in my life. I knew you couldn't choose your family but if I was given the chance I'd choose all of them again.

Mum started to explain the finer points of the contract when there was a terrible commotion as we heard wood splintering in the wake of a size 11 Doctor Marten's boot.

Aunt Delia burst into the room. As my new security person, Uncle Terry jumped up and covered me with his mac.

'Oh no!' Aunt Delia moaned, 'I'm too late!'

'Nonsense,' I cried, throwing off the mac and looking at our smashed door. 'Family is family. There's more tea in the pot and I feel so energised by this get-together that I might nip out to the corner store and buy a marble cake or some Battenburg.'

Uncle Terry stood up. 'Aunt Delia,' he said.

'Uncle Terry,' she replied.

'Where's Uncle Cedric?' I asked.

'He has a prior engagement,' she explained, 'something to do with chilblains.'

'Okay, everyone, let's keep calm,' Dad said.

But Aunt Delia didn't let him finish. 'After all that trouble down south, David came to me and I looked after him like my own son. Admittedly I looked after my own son pretty badly, but that's irrelevant. I want in with this deal. It's my right.'

The tension in the room crackled like the oil in a griddle pan.

Mum, Dad and Uncle Terry formed a small huddle and whispered amongst themselves for five minutes.

Then Mum looked up and nodded sagely. 'You're in,' she said to Aunt Delia.

Dad looked resigned and hurriedly added a couple of lines to the contract. Aunt Delia inspected them closely with her monocle. She pulled out her mobile and quickly dialled her phone-a-friend – an elderly lady in Crumpsall, who possessed a remarkable general knowledge and specialised in the making and arrangement of paper doilies. After a conversation about hi-fi separates, they got serious. Aunt Delia didn't actually speak during this next bit – she just nodded her head emphatically. She then flicked her phone shut.

'The terms are acceptable,' she said.

It was as if a balloon had suddenly been burst. The atmosphere changed instantly from *Gunfight at the OK Corral* to *The Cat in the Hat*.

I wrapped my arms around myself. I couldn't believe these people cared so much about me.

'I can't take much more of this,' muttered Vivian to me, pulling on a trench-coat and heading out through what was left of the door. 'I'll be back in a couple of hours,' she hissed, 'make sure they're gone by then.'

I tried to kiss her on the cheek but missed and performed an air kiss. No one noticed, though, so it was fine. I totally understood where Vivian was coming from. They were *my* family and she wanted to give me some space alone with them. As soon as she'd gone, Dad started talking.

'Where do you keep earnings accrued through media appearances and any related business activities?' he asked.

The guy was priceless – always worried about my financial stability.

'It's cool, Dad,' I replied, 'we're doing fine. Television pays surprisingly well and the papers have coughed up for lots of the photos.'

'How much?' asked Mum.

'Well, *Robert and Julie* was—'

'Spare us the details, David,' Uncle Terry said firmly. 'We just need the cumulative pot.'

I looked blank for a few seconds and then scrawled down a sum on a blank piece of paper and shoved it across the table in his direction.

Uncle Terry studied the figure and handed it round the others.

'Where's it kept?' asked Clare.

'It's in a high-interest account with the Nottingham and Purley Way Building Society,' I replied.

'Account number?' asked Mum.

I fetched my wallet, pulled out a card and shared the information.

'Sort code?' asked Aunt Delia.

I read it out from the card.

'Good work, son,' beamed Dad. 'We'll be back in an hour.'

And with that, they all left. By the time Vivian returned they hadn't reappeared. She asked me what I'd talked to them about. When I said I'd told them about the building society account, she flipped.

'YOU TOLD THEM WHAT?' she screamed.

'Chill out,' I said.

But she didn't hear me. She was dialling the Nottingham

and Purley Way Building Society. The call lasted no more than a minute.

'They've cleaned us out,' she said quietly.

'What are you talking about?'

'Your family. They've fleeced us. You've signed away all of our savings to them.'

I laughed heartily at this preposterous notion.

'No, Vivian. They haven't fleeced us. They've only taken the money to reinvest it on our behalf. Japanese equities are looking particularly promising at the minute.'

'NO, DAVID! They haven't reinvested our money. They won't be buying Japanese equities or high-income bonds or even hedge funds. THEY'VE NICKED IT!'

I didn't respond. Vivian had been up for the last three nights because of the baby and it was clearly taking its toll on her. Just yesterday I'd seen her holding an animated conversation with a Farley's rusk. She didn't know my family like I did. They were rock solid. They'd found me. They were protecting me. They were looking out for *us*.

Vivian was furious with me over the money situation for weeks, but I kept telling her it would be okay. We'd get our pot of gold at the end of the rainbow, I assured her.

It was a funny old time, what with Vivian's outbursts and the press attention. I could see how people got caught up in the great merry-go-round of fame. It's exciting and enticing. And the booze comes on tap. But I knew where my priorities lay. And when Chorlton-Cum-Hardy got cradle cap, I saw everything totally clearly.

Vivian was struggling to apply all of the correct lotions to his hair and begged me to miss training one morning.

'Give me a couple of minutes,' I said softly.

I dialled the number of Reeves McManan – Sralex Ferfuson's right-hand man.

After a few rings, it went on to answerphone.

'This is David Feckham,' I said. 'I need to speak to you, Reevesy, or the gaffer himself.'

They must have been screening, because a few seconds later our phone rang.

It was Sralex. 'We were screening,' he said.

I gulped nervously.

'Boss, I need to talk to you about training today.'

'Yes?' His phone manner was often quite concise.

'Chorlton-Cum-Hardy's a bit under the weather and I was wondering if—'

He didn't even let me finish the sentence.

'Of course, David. You're doing the right thing. Miss training today to be with your wife and son. It's where you should be. In fact, you can miss the next month of training if you want to. No one's indispensable, especially y—'

But I didn't let him finish. I carried the phone to the other side of the flat and lowered my voice. 'No, boss,' I whispered, 'you've got it all wrong. I'm desperate to get *out*. If you say I have to turn up for training it will be a perfect excuse for me to get away. Vivian will take it from you.'

There was a pause as Sralex mulled this over.

'You irresponsible little shit,' he eventually said. 'In a time of declining social values and a lack of morally acceptable boundaries, it's more crucial than ever that you conform to some basic standards of familial integration.'

'So you'll cover for me?' I asked.

'No, David!' Sralex barked. 'I will not cover for you. And I'll make it bloody hard for you to get here, so don't even think about it!'

I don't know what it was that pushed me over the edge – but it could have been the poor reception on our new digital phone. I sauntered back towards Vivian who was rubbing parmesan into Chorlton-Cum-Hardy's hair.

'Well?' she asked, looking at me expectantly. 'What did he say?'

I pursed my lips in that sympathetic way that doctors do, when they're about to tell you some really bad news. 'The gaffer says I'm irreplaceable. He needs me there.'

Vivian looked at me with shock. 'Please tell me you're joking, David.'

'Straight up,' I replied. 'He says the whole thing can't function properly without me.'

Vivian sighed heavily. 'Well if that's the way it is, I suppose I'll just have to accept it,' she said, 'but as soon as training is over, come straight home.'

'Of course,' I said, stooping down to kiss her, while crossing the fingers of my right hand behind my back.

I got my bag, hurried out of the flat and got in the car. I turned right and headed towards the high street. At the first junction there was a lollipop lady ushering children across the road. But when all of the kids had gone, she stood on the zebra crossing directly in front of me holding her lollipop threateningly and directing me to turn round. What the hell was she playing at? *I'll show her*, I thought to myself. I reversed a few metres and sped across to the other side of the road, whizzing past her and narrowly avoiding a box van delivering staples to an industrial park.

A mile on and the lane I usually cut through was lined with work signs, saying NO ENTRY – ROAD BEING REBUILT. I saw ahead of me that a great hole had been dug in the centre of the road, completely barring access. But I'd seen loads of action films and went for the 'flyer'. I accelerated to eighty miles an hour and used two planks as my lift-off. Remarkably it worked, even though the car looped the loop and lost its exhaust pipe on the descent.

When I reached the bottom of the hill leading directly up to the training ground, I came across a massive roadblock.

There were huge stone blocks and razor wire strung out across the road, on either side of a small sentry box and a red and white barrier. A guy wearing a flak jacket walked over, leant down and told me to open my window.

'Sorry, mate – you need to turn back,' he told me.

The rational part of me knew that I should follow this army guy's instructions, but the other part of me thought *fuck you!* So I just put my foot down. The car smashed through the wooden barrier as the army man leapt out of the way.

As I drove my battered car into the training ground car park, Sralex was waiting for me, holding the leashes of six bloodhounds, all growling and all muzzled. The entire first team squad were standing behind him with pencils and clipboards at the ready.

'Look and learn, lads,' said Sralex. 'Look and learn.' Then he eyed me with contempt.

'What did I tell you, David?' he muttered, loosening his grip on the dogs' leashes. 'Where did I say you should be?'

For a second I was confused. Was this a multipart question or was a single answer sufficient? And could I use a calculator?

'Why didn't you read the "signs" on the way?' he continued. 'Angela is one of the city's finest kung-fu lollipop women and you ignored her. I had that road specially dug up and you ignored it. And the army officer is my wife's third cousin and you bypassed him. What will it take for you to toe the line, David?'

We were both really angry by now. Him in a loud, boiling, out there kind of way. Me in a tender, reflective, within myself kind of way. I paused as I tried to outthink him.

'You have a lovely wife at home with an ill child and yet you decided to come here,' he said with a sneer.

'You leave Vivian out of it,' I shouted. 'How would you feel if I started mouthing off about how lovely your wife is?'

This clearly puzzled him, as his lips moved but no words came out.

I looked from the gaffer's face to the frenzied snarling of the dogs and on to the expectant faces of my team-mates, who were scribbling furiously on their pads. Some of their pencils had already gone blunt and they were passing sharpeners between themselves.

I stared at Sralex for a few more seconds and then eased myself back into my car. I turned around and jolted out of the car park. The lack of an exhaust pipe might prove a problem on the way home, I thought.

As I drove, my rage increased. At times, Sralex had been like a real father figure to me, a guiding hand, an inspiration. But this outburst of his had crossed the line, particularly as it occurred in front of the rest of the players.

We'd had words before but this was totally different. This wasn't some normal day-to-day dressing down.

This time it was personal.

CHAPTER 9:

Captain Fantastic (Not the Elton John album)

'Ugh, sweaty.'

They say fate is a funny old thing, but I prefer to think that destiny is quite amusing. My run-in with the gaffer could have left a nasty taste in the mouth, a bit like when you eat some curry and accidentally bite on a bay leaf you hadn't realised was there. My relationship with Mr Ferfuson had definitely changed over the years. He had become more distant, sometimes standing half a kilometre away when talking to me. On other days he preferred to communicate with me telepathically. Don't get me wrong, I still loved him, I just wasn't sure I was *in* love with him any longer. But then fate played its hand. I found out about it first from Brevilley.

'Have you heard?' he said to me on the fourteenth hole of our local crazy golf course.

I looked at my caddy and shrugged.

'Heard what?' I enquired.

'They reckon Mr Ferfuson has had enough – he's going to call it a day.'

I couldn't believe it. I teed off with a three wood – a mistake in retrospect. The ball flew straight into one of the sails of the windmill on the fairway and rebounded back to my feet.

'Now look what you've made me do,' I said. 'So who's going to take over?'

'I don't know,' Brevilley said. Then he looked at me with a mixture of what I can only describe as languor and utter despair.

'And there's something else as well,' he said. 'You know the new manager of the England Pub Sunday League team? They reckon he could be . . .' He paused for dramatic effect. Twenty minutes later he eventually said, '. . . a foreigner.'

That was almost too much. Mr Ferfuson was one thing, but a foreigner taking over the England Pub Sunday League team? That was two things. My head was full of unanswered questions like What's the capital of Nicaragua? How do bees actually make honey? And what is the cube root of 317?

Back in the pub the talk was all about Mr Ferfuson, apart from two old women sitting in the corner, who were discussing eggs. Everyone knew he had a fifty per cent share in a water polo player and that for a while now he'd been spending more and more time at the local Olympic-sized swimming pool. Perhaps that was where he saw his future lying.

From my point of view I had mixed emotions, congealed feelings if you like. I wondered if perhaps his decision might have something to do with our relationship, so I decided to ring him.

'Hello, gaffer, it's me, David Feckham.'

'Where the hell are you?' he shouted.

'I'm in the pub with the lads,' I said.

'Don't lie to me,' he screamed. 'You're in Birmingham – a mate's just seen you coming out of Agent Provocateur in the Bullring.'

That made no sense at all, but just to be on the safe side I double-checked my surroundings. There was no sexy lingerie anywhere to be seen.

'Honestly, gaffer,' I said, 'there aren't any silk cami knickers, teddies or crotchless panties anywhere. I'm definitely not in Birmingham.'

'Listen,' he said, 'pick me up a peephole bra and we'll say no more about it, all right?'

Then he hung up.

I didn't know what to make of it, but I got Vivian to take her bra off and cut a hole in each cup nonetheless. Five minutes later I was pleased I'd done so, and not just because I could now see her nipples. Mr Ferfuson's silhouette appeared in the doorway of the pub. A hushed silence fell over the place. He strode in, coming to a stop in the centre of the room. All eyes fell upon him. He cleared his throat and adjusted his tie. Then he did up his shoelaces and combed his hair before blowing his nose and cutting his fingernails. Finally he spoke.

'There's been a lot of talk,' he said, 'and some sign language, about my future. Well I'm here to put the record straight.'

A buzz went round the room; a wasp had got in through a window.

'This will be my last season as manager of The Schnitzel and Parrot senior team. I'm retiring next summer.'

It was the bombshell that we'd all been expecting, but it still hurt when it hit. At first no one knew what to say. Then Uncle Cedric broke the ice.

'Pint please, Spike,' he said, 'with a quadruple rum chaser.'

Slowly the pub returned to normal as people began digesting the news, then regurgitating it in the same way a camel might chew the cud. The talk was all about who might take over, apart from the two old ladies in the corner who were now discussing bath salts.

'What do you reckon?' I said to Brevilley, who had taken the news badly and was curled up in a ball in the corner of the room, gently rocking and sobbing.

'I don't know,' he said between sobs, 'and I don't care.'

He was so emotional, the slightest little thing would set him off.

'I reckon we're going to get that geezer from The Offset Mortgage and Doppelganger,' said Puttsy.

'No way,' countered Miggsy. 'He couldn't manage an apple on an empty stomach.'

I wasn't sure if that metaphor worked, but I let it go. I was just about to throw in my twopennyworth, when the gaffer himself started to wander over. What would he have to say on the matter? As a group we all tensed up, then, to relax a little, gave each other a quick shiatsu massage. Mr Ferfuson approached the table.

'Now, Fecks, I believe you have something for me?' he said.

That was the gaffer all over, carrying on as if nothing untoward had happened.

'Yes, boss,' I said and handed him Vivian's bra.

'Still warm, mmmmm,' he said, nuzzling the soft white material to his cheek.

It was good to see that he was still his old self, but part of me knew things weren't right, whilst another part of me wondered if Mr Ferfuson might know more about things disappearing from our washing line than he'd previously let on.

On the international scene things were still very much up in the air. The rumours about the new manager of the England Pub Sunday League team turned out to be true: he was a foreigner. Nobody knew exactly where he was from – a foreign land no doubt, but how would his being a foreigner affect the team? Would his methods seem alien to us peace-loving island-dwelling folk? It was a big question, possibly *the* big question, and it definitely had an impact on my game. What with that and Mr Ferfuson's impending retirement, I just couldn't concentrate. I felt like I was floating around the pitch for the opening few games that season, not really there, but not really anywhere else either.

On many an occasion I would actually sit on the halfway line in the pose of Rodin's famous statue, *The Thinker*, and do just that – sit. It wasn't too bad because you can't be offside unless you're in your opponents' half and I was always careful to be right on the line. As a tactic it seemed to work quite well in fact, as our opponents would often send two, even three players to mark me, giving our front men far more freedom.

Generally, though, the whole team seemed affected by everything that was going on off the pitch and our form was erratic: one week we'd lose three–nil and the very next Saturday we'd lose four–nil. It was mad.

Then ten games into the season we got the call.

'The new England boss, that foreigner,' said Mr Ferfuson one day after training, 'he wants to have a get-together with the squad.'

A murmur of approval jostled through the team.

'I've told him Brevilley, Miggsy, Puttsy and Scooby are injured,' continued Mr Ferfuson, 'but you can go, Fecks.'

Brevilley, Miggsy, Puttsy and Scooby looked at each other. They weren't injured, but they knew what was coming. Mr Ferfuson knew exactly where he stood in the pub v country debate. For the next three weeks at least, whenever they were out in public they'd all be wearing plaster casts, eyepatches and surgical stockings.

As for me I was deeply honoured not to have been chosen to have to pretend to be injured. It was yet another example of how highly I was regarded. As Miggsy squeezed into his stocking, I smiled inwardly to myself, whilst outwardly grimacing, not at all an easy thing to do.

Meeting up with the other England boys is always exciting. When you play against those lads week in week out they are the enemy. You hate them with a passion and wish that they'd lose both legs in a horrific accident. But that's all forgotten in the England set-up. They become your mates. Past history is just that, past and history.

This time of course it was even more exciting because we were meeting the new manager for the first time. It turned out his name was Mr Ben Turd Vodaphone. He was wearing loud check trousers, had a plastic policeman's hat on his head and was handing out leaflets for English language courses; there was no doubt in my mind that he was foreign. From the moment he first spoke I knew we were going to get on.

'Goodbye it was nicest not to meet them,' he said. His English was astonishingly good for a foreigner from foreign climes. He then proceeded to give us a team talk that went on for nine hours. As a student of the beautiful game I was fascinated. Not only that, by the end, I was the only one still awake.

'Goods,' he said. 'So, questions any thank you table.'

I racked my brain. If I could ask a really good question, one that showed I'd been listening intently throughout, that surely would cement our relationship. I raised my hand meekly. He glanced quickly at an English/Inuit, Inuit/Flemish dictionary.

'No,' he said.

'Yes,' I corrected.

He tutted and proceeded to feed the dictionary through a paper-shredder.

'Yes,' he said.

'Can you spell Beckenbauer?' I asked.

He looked at me for a moment. I studied his mouth. Which way would the corners turn? Upwards into a smile or downwards into a snarl? For a moment I thought one corner might turn up and the other down in a sort of snarlsmile, or scowlsmirk, but then both corners simultaneously rolled on up and I knew the cement had dried on our relationship.

Over the next few days I worked on my staying-awake techniques. It was a challenge: Mr Vodaphone's talks were getting longer and more detailed, and he seemed to have perfected a voice that was somewhere between a monotone and a drone, but by having coffee intravenously delivered to my veins, I was just able to fend off sleep. And at the end of the get-together I was rewarded for my effort in spades.

'Fecks,' said Mr Vodaphone. 'You Cuba Gooding Jnr listener. This is hairy important marmalade.'

'Why thank you, Mr Vodaphone,' I said, my eyelids fighting to close, but failing due to the superglue that was holding them open.

What happened next is something I'll never forget as long as I live and for at least my next eight lives after that. Mr Vodaphone knelt down and, from a ruby and shallot-encrusted box that he kept handcuffed to his ankle, produced an armband. He tossed it into my lap.

'Captain my captain,' he said; clearly he'd seen *Dead Poets Society* without subtitles in his country, wherever that was.

At first, though, I assumed his English was failing him.

Surely he's not asking me to be captain? I thought. But slowly the truth dawned on me, like the sun rising over a hillside on a dewy, Devonshire morning in late autumn. I,

David Feckham, was going to captain my country, England. If it hadn't been for the superglue I would have rubbed my eyes and blinked over and over to check I wasn't dreaming. It was such an honour. I couldn't believe it. I wanted to shout it from the rooftops, to tell the whole world, but I knew that would wake the others so I had to keep it bottled for the time being.

Back in my room I was still groggy from the excitement of it all. I wanted to phone Vivian, Mum, Dad, Uncle Terry, Delia, Chorlton-Cum-Hardy, Uncle Cedric and, for some reason, Sir Ranulph Fiennes. In the end it came down to a toss-up between Vivian and Sir Ranulph. Vivian won.

'Viv,' I shouted breathlessly down the phone.

'Who is this?' came the response.

I'd forgotten I'd been away from home for a couple of days.

'It's me, David, remember, your husband.'

'Oh yeah right, got you. So what do you want?'

'I'm captain, I've been made captain of England.' The words shot out of me like tennis balls being fired out of one of those machines that fire out tennis balls.

'That's nice. Now listen, David, I'm releasing my first solo single this weekend, you will be back for it, won't you?'

'Course, love, how's Chorl—'

But she was gone. Or I had been cut off. Or both. But it didn't matter. All that mattered was that I was captain. Me, me, me, me, me, me, me, me, me, and especially me. Oh, and me.

The following day I was still basking in the glory of it all, walking tall, erect, proud. I felt like the last man in that picture of man's evolution, you know, the one where we evolve from apes and in each successive image are walking more and more upright. But once I got home it was a different story and I had to devolve somewhat. Viv was in a right mess about her forthcoming single release. Nervous wasn't the word for it. She was narvous.

She'd made the record with the help of an old friend from the Copycats days, Slyman Fullahimself. They'd had five hundred copies of the single, a Euro-funk garage version of 'Who Do You Think You Are Kidding Mr Hitler', pressed in purple vinyl and had delivered it personally to all the radio stations, clubs, pubs, bars, and pawnshops in the area. They were hoping it would become a massive underground hit and then go on to be a huge mainstream hit and then be used in an advert for Pepsi or a flash car. It just needed the airplay, which was why, the day after its release, we were all gathered around the radio, listening out for that first syncopated drumbeat.

Viv gingerly moved the dial, not wanting to miss any radio station no matter if it was pirate or even Greek. An hour later we hadn't heard those beats. Two hours later and still nothing. Another hour later and we were just about to give up the ghost when we heard them booming, well crackling, out of the small hand-held transistor radio. We all cheered then listened intently.

'That was our tune of the week, "Who Do You Think You Are Kidding Mr Hitler" by Vivian Feckham,' said the DJ.

We couldn't believe it. Me captain of England and now Viv's single was tune of the week. Slyman broke open the champagne; the cork nearly took Chorlton-Cum-Hardy's eye out. We listened again to the DJ.

'Righty oh,' he said. 'Now it's time for one of our very favourite sections here on Hospital Radio Nettleton: "Before I Die", where you lucky terminally ill people get to choose a final song before—'

Vivian turned the radio off. The look on her face said it all, but I still checked to make sure.

'You all right love?' I ventured tentatively.

Before she could answer Slyman picked the radio up and flung it out of the window with all his might. It was a silly thing to do as it left us with no radio, and the window was shut at the time, but I knew how he felt.

'Don't worry, darling,' I said, 'even the Beatles had to start somewhere.'

She looked at me, great African-elephant tears streaming down her cheeks.

'Who the fuck are the Beatles?' she said.

And to be fair, she had a point.

Over the next few days Vivian went into a shell. She'd crawl around the bedsit under it and talked about hibernating during the winter and *Blue Peter*. It cost us a fortune in lettuce, but I wasn't worried about her. I knew she was made of strong stuff and wouldn't let one knockback knock her back.

My attentions now turned back to my role as captain of England. I hadn't taken that armband off since Mr Vodaphone gave it to me, even though it was quite tight and was restricting blood flow to my fingers. After the first rush of excitement, I'd had a chance to let things sink in a bit, and, sitting in the lavatory having a dump one day, I realised something was missing. What I needed was an agent. All the big names had one and what was I now if not a big name? I had no doubt that getting one wouldn't be a problem; to be honest I was surprised I hadn't been approached already.

My mind made up, I decided to act immediately. However, something else was missing. Toilet paper. It was a problem and I'm not proud of what happened next; it's not for these pages, but there are times when you just have to make do.

Half an hour and a clean pair of socks later I was on the phone to every agent in the book. The first nineteen turned me down point blank. I couldn't understand it until I realised they were all travel agents or estate agents. I fared marginally better with the next twelve, but clearly word of my captaincy hadn't seeped out yet and I met with polite but firm refusals. The next forty-six went the same way, as did the next twenty-eight and the next seventy-two, but then I rang Teeny Weeny Mata Hari Uberagents to the Stars Ltd. Here's how the conversation went.

'Hello Teeny Weeny Mata Hari Uberagents to the Stars Ltd. How can we be of assistance to you?'

'This is David Feckham, captain of the England Pub Sunday League team,' I said, 'I'm looking for an agent.'

'All our lines are busy right now but if you'd care to leave a message someone will definitely get back to you as soon as is humanly possible.'

Wow I thought. *They're going to get back to me. They want me. I have an agent.*

It was as simple as that. I was so chuffed, I bought myself a small packet of Trill to celebrate.

The other lads couldn't believe it.

'Nice one, Cap,' said Puttsy. They'd started calling me Cap since I'd been made captain, not because I'd changed my name by deed poll or anything, but because it was short for captain.

'Yeah, El Capitano, you're a player now, in the big league,' said Miggsy. (They'd also started calling me El Capitano for some reason.)

'Thanks, guys,' I said, 'but I don't want this to change anything between us, okay? We're still mates, right?'

'Course we are,' said Brevilley, looking up from the floor where he was shining my shoes.

'Good. Now then, I was thinking about a mascot for the forthcoming match against Spain. I reckon Chorlton-Cum-Hardy might be just right for it. What do you reckon?'

They all agreed it was the best idea since granary bread and so did I. Me and my boy leading out the England team, could life get any better?

The day of the match came round and Chorlton-Cum-Hardy, still suffering from the vestiges of cradle cap, but having passed a late fitness test, was next to me in the tunnel, waiting to lead our country on to the field of play. He'd already done me proud by staying awake during Mr Vodaphone's three-hour pre-match team talk that had included a slide show and mime troupe from Tonga. Now I was so proud I could have burst and knowing that Vivian was in the stands to see it all only added to my pride and sense of bursting. I held his little hand tightly as we walked out on to the pitch.

'Ugh, sweaty,' he said, yanking it away and wiping the excess perspiration on my shorts.

I smiled. He was so like Vivian.

I tossed a ball to him. He chested it down, dribbled round three Spanish players and then planted it perfectly in the bottom right-hand corner of their net. It was the weirdest feeling, watching him. He reminded me so much of a young me, though not as cute, or as talented of course. As he trotted back over grinning cheekily from nostril to nostril, my heart sang.

'One–nil to us, eh Dad?' he said.

'Now, Chorlton-Cum-Hardy, remember what I said, this is only the pre-match kickabout, the game hasn't actually started, yeah?'

'What! You're having a laugh aren't you? I scored fair and square. Oi, ref . . .'

Next thing I knew he was having it large with the ref, an Armenian fellow who taught balloon modelling for a living.

'Chorlton-Cum-Hardy!' I shouted, but it was too late.

I watched in horror as the ref reached into his breast pocket.

'Let it be yellow, let it be yellow,' I prayed.

But to no avail.

'Off,' screamed the ref holding aloft a red card.

Chorlton-Cum-Hardy's face went white. He turned and walked back to the tunnel, taking off his shirt and throwing it angrily to the ground as he did so. It was quite a blow and meant he'd be suspended from being mascot for the next four games. I looked up and searched for Vivian's face in the stands. Fortunately she was deeply involved in a game of Cat's Cradle with the Spanish ambassador's personal envoy and had missed it all.

The game itself was pretty uneventful. We won. Or lost. I can't remember exactly. I do remember that I did a good job as captain. When the lads' heads looked like dropping I took a selection of latticed pastries round to perk them up, which did the trick.

After the game I attended the post-match press conference with Mr Vodaphone. He took fourteen hours to answer the first question, and even then managed to say a lot without really saying anything at all. He was a master at dealing with the ladies and gentlemen of the press.

Later that night I rang my agent to find out if any endorsement work had come in. The heating in our building was playing up and I was particularly keen to lend my name to any radiator or central-heating manufacturers.

'Thank you for calling the offices of Teeny Weeny Mata Hari Uberagents to the Stars Ltd,' the same voice as before said.

'Oh hello, it's David Feckham here, I just wondered if you could sort me out some endorsements—'

'All our lines are busy right now,' continued the voice.

'But if you'd care to leave a message someone will definitely get back to you as soon as humanly possible. Beep.'

With that sorted, I put the phone down.

It felt great to have an agent.

I felt certain that before too long, fame and truckloads of cash would be trundling down Rue Feckham.

CHAPTER 10:

Fighting Unfit

'I've been told I can play, on crutches.'

Someone once asked me what I'd do if football didn't exist.

'What would you do if football didn't exist?' they asked me.

Quick as a flash I said, 'I'd pursue a career as an actuary.'

It was a good answer, but to be honest I don't know what I'd really do if football didn't exist. It's always been there for me; we're joined at the hip. The nearest we've ever come to separating is when I got injured. That was a tough time for me, and for football.

The injury came not long after two highly significant events in the 2001/2002 season. The first was our final World Cup qualifying game against Greece. The Greeks are not really a pub nation, preferring small bars and tavernas on the whole, so we were expected to give them a trouncing and win the match as well, something that would see us reach the World Cup finals in style as group winners. If we drew we'd have to wait and see what happened in the Germany v Finland match that was being played simultaneously. If we lost we'd be at the mercy of what happened in the Lithuania v Faroe Islands game that was being played simultaneously, but in a parallel universe.

Then of course there was the possibility that if we were winning at half time, but Germany were drawing with Finland and Lithuania were winning, we would go into a play-off with the half-time losers of Italy and the Domini-can Republic. I could go on, but suffice to say the permutations were endless. We just had to win.

The game itself was a tense, yet exciting affair. There were periods when we played some great flowing football, and others when we played some great flowing cricket. With three nanoseconds to go, though, we were a goal down and heading for the play-offs. Then we got a free kick just outside their box. Freddy Sheriff of Nottingham stepped up to take it.

'I'll have this one,' I said to him.

'Like fuck you will, this is mine,' he said.

Well, as captain I couldn't let such insubordination go unpunished. It might have been seen as weakness and lead to a mutiny. I picked up the ball, shoved it under my shirt and ran.

'You want it, you come and get it then, you big bollock,' I shouted.

Freddy charged after me like a marauding wildebeest. Then all the other players, both Greek and English, started after me. Before long I was lying beneath an enormous mound of writhing football players. It seemed unlikely that I'd get to take the free kick, but then I saw a small gap just between their left back and Puttsy. I made my bid for freedom and before anyone knew it I was away and in on goal. I placed the ball down and went to curl it beautifully into the top left-hand corner. In fact I stubbed my toe as I was running in on it, but the resultant toe punt still just about crawled over the line and into the empty net.

Running off celebrating the goal was an amazing moment, even Freddy came over and congratulated me, though his pat on the back was a little on the rough side – nearer to a punch really.

The crowd were going wild and I knew Germany must

have been losing/drawing/winning against Finland/Bermuda/Laos and we were through/out/in the play-offs. I just stood there and drank it all in. Then I caught sight of Vivian. She also seemed ecstatic and was unfurling a large banner. I expected it to say something like, 'David I love you', or maybe, 'David I really like you', but I couldn't believe it when I read, 'David I'm pregnant again'. I have to say it was an odd way to tell me the news, but it only added to what was already an amazing moment.

In the bedsit that evening I lay on the bed with Vivian and Chorlton-Cum-Hardy.

'What a day,' I said.

'Yeah,' said Vivian. 'How about a night out to celebrate?'

'Okay,' I vouchsafed. 'Where shall we go?'

'How about the pub?' she said.

I was amazed. She was just so full of great ideas. Before you could say, 'Curry Motors nice people to do business with,' we'd got one of the less psychotic neighbours (Oona – a watchmaker who couldn't tell the time) to babysit Chorlton-Cum-Hardy. Then it was on with the glad rags and down to the boozer.

It was quiz night that evening and together with the lads we formed a team that went by the humorous moniker 'Bright Guys'. We came second, narrowly losing to 'The Brains In Spain', who were playing via a satellite link-up from Seville. They won a tube of Bostik. We weren't disappointed at losing, though – the day had been incredible enough already. But there was still one more surprise in store.

Just as the quizmaster, Bamber Shillingforthemeter, was packing the microphone away, Mr Ferfuson walked into the pub.

'I'll have that, Bamber,' he said assertively.

Bamber instantly acquiesced.

All eyes, ears, noses and mouths fell upon Mr Ferfuson. 'I'm staying on,' was all he said.

There was confusion all round the pub. Did he mean he was staying on in his council flat? Or in his position as a sales rep for a firm of salad-tong manufacturers? Or did he in fact mean that he was staying on that very spot where he was currently standing? Clearly he sensed the bewilderment as his next statement cleared the matter up.

'As manager of the pub football team.'

There was a moment of intense silence, then everyone in the pub cheered and threw their hats in the air as if they were at a football match in the 1950s. It was a moment I'll never forget. This man had been a father, a brother, an uncle, a nanny, an au pair, a cleaner and a wet nurse for us all for so long. It meant everything that he was staying on. Brevilley, me, Scooby, Puttsy and Miggsy hugged each other and then, still arm in arm, Cossack danced over to him.

'Great news, boss,' said Scooby, using up his daily word allowance in one go.

'Yeah,' said Miggsy, 'if you'd retired I don't know what I might have done, probably just sat at home and eaten Gouda cheese for days on end, staring aimlessly at the walls.'

'Well, I'm pleased then,' said Mr Ferfuson, 'because that's one sure-fire way to get gout.'

As for me, I was pleased that the boss was staying on, but I had to admit that it was tempered with displeasure as well, so much so that I couldn't actually feel any pleasure about it at all. I congratulated him of course, but the way he hugged me felt unreal, as if his hands were hugging my throat really tightly. I decided to call my agent.

'Thank you for calling the offices of Teeny Weeny Mata Hari Uberagents to the Stars Ltd,' the now familiar voice said. This time I knew better than to interrupt.

'All our lines are busy right now. But if you'd care to leave a message someone will definitely get back to you as soon as humanly possible. Beep.'

Then I just unloaded. Let it all out. It felt great. They let me go on for twenty minutes. At the end I felt much better. It's a very rare skill to be able to listen, properly, but my agent had it, and I was overjoyed about that.

Returning to the bedsit we paid the not-so-psychotic babysitter, £3.91 an hour plus expenses which came to £75.67, and crashed down on the bed, exhausted. I expected to be asleep within seconds, but Vivian had other ideas. Before I knew what was happening she was licking my hair seductively.

'Stop it, Viv,' I said coyly.

But it was too late, blood was gushing to my penis in great torrents. I rolled over into the masonry position and prepared to enter Vivian's love bucket.

'Hang on,' she said.

I hung on.

'Aren't you forgetting something?'

I couldn't think what she might be referring to, so I made a face that I hoped said, *Huh?*

'The condom, silly,' said Viv.

'But Viv,' I said, 'we don't need one, you're pregnant.'

'I know,' she said, 'but I don't want to get pregnant again, do I? Not so soon.'

She was right, I didn't want *two* more children. I got out of bed and tiptoed over to the cabinet where we kept the condoms and various other sex-related objects such as dildos, vibrators, giant strap-on cockies and the like. It was dark and I was being careful not to step on any of Chorlton-Cum-Hardy's toys, but as I manoeuvred round his Junior Toll Booth Operator's Kit, I failed to see his Noon Chucks lying to one side. As I placed a bare foot on them they gave way and sent me flying to the ground. I instantly cried out in agony.

'Aaaaaaaarrrrrrrrrgggggggggggggggghhhhhhhhhhhh!' I said. 'My foot.'

I knew immediately that something was very wrong. My little toe had wrapped itself around my ankle and my big toe was hanging limply from beneath the middle of my sole. Four hour later my worst fears were confirmed.

'If I had a penny for every Junior Toll Booth Operator's Kit and Noon Chuck related injury we have in here,' said the junior doctor in casualty, 'I'd be a rich man. You've broken a number of bones in your foot. You won't be walking again for a while.'

'But will I be able to play football, doc?' I asked pleading like a puppy dog.

The doctor looked at me, sighed, then shook his head, which I took to mean no.

After I'd had another eight opinions the truth began to dawn on me: I was injured. Unselfishly my first thoughts weren't to do with me or my family, they were to do with the team. How would they cope without their lynchpin, the midfield general, their God?

I rang Mr Ferfuson.

'Boss, I've got some bad news,' I said.

'Don't tell me,' he said, 'you've found out that you're not Chorlton-Cum-Hardy's father.'

'No, much worse than that. I've broken some bones in my foot. I won't be able to play football for a while. I might not even make the World Cup.'

There was silence on the other end of the line, but I felt sure he was stifling a sob.

'Boss? Boss?' I said. 'Speak to me.'

But he was gone. All I could hear was the Brazilian samba music he'd put on to cover his weeping.

That first night I lay in bed unable to even make it to the pub for a hastily arranged party someone had organised for that evening. I tried to lose myself in football magazines, *442*, *Total Football*, *Waterways World* and the like, but it was no good. Reading about football is a poor substitute for playing football, as any professional footballer who has gone on to be a professional reader will tell you.

The next couple of months were pure, unadulterated hell. Vivian had morning sickness and was freestyle vomiting into every container we possessed. She actually developed it into quite an art and was able to projectile vomit into an empty can of baked beans from twenty yards away. Chorlton-Cum-Hardy was going through the terrible twos, even though he was now three. He'd throw tantrum after tantrum after tantrum, which in effect is tantrum before tantrum before tantrum. Sometimes they were over the most trivial of things, such as my contention that Kant's *General Natural History and Theory of the Heavens* is, historically, a more important book than *The Critique of Pure Reason*. And in the middle of it all, with my injury, was me.

It felt like a life sentence where life means life with no possibility of parole. My mail was censored and I could only speak to visitors via a telephone from the other side of a glass panel. The only respite I got was football on the telly. We had Sky, Sky+, Sky Extra, Sky Extra+, Sky+ Extra, Extra Sky Extra, Extra+Sky+Extra+, Sky Mix+, Sky+ExtraMix+Mix-Extra and Men and Motors, so I was able to watch some game or other for twenty-three hours and forty-eight minutes of every day, but those twelve minutes where all I could watch was Sky News's *Football Latest* show nearly did for me.

Medically I was in the best possible hands. A couple of regulars from The Schnitzel and Parrot were fully trained witch doctors. They prescribed a combination of healing herbs that I made into a poultice every night and wrapped around my elbow – apparently in witch doctory the elbow is the part of the body that represents the foot. It wasn't always easy getting hold of gnu's toenail clippings and sea cucumber's dandruff, our local Tesco's was often out of the stuff, but I always managed to find some and by six each evening was sitting, as instructed, facing due north by north north in an indigo basque chanting an ancient healing prayer. It wasn't a bad tune actually. It went: 'Ni Supma Thab Rown, Ni Supma Thab Rown, Ni Sup, Ni Sup, Gottagetyo Ni Sup, Ni Supma Thab Rown.'

Of course I was on the phone to Mr Vodaphone every day with updates regarding my progress. His English was improving rapidly and sometimes I could almost understand ten per cent of what he was saying.

Then, with one week to our opening World Cup game, just when I thought I'd never look at a football ever again, let alone kick one, I got the message I wanted to hear. It came via semaphore and told me I was in the clear. I immediately rang Mr Vodaphone.

'Mr Vodaphone, it's David Feckham, I've been told I can play, on crutches.'

It was the news he and the whole country had been waiting for. I'd go so far as to say that Mr Vodaphone even coughed a little, which for a man as tortuously dull as him, was tantamount to jumping for joy, stripping down to his bare essentials and eating a large marrow.

Mr Ferfuson was also delighted. The pub team had done their best without me, but they had really struggled to win every game. 'Course the lads had a joke and a laugh about it. Some of them even pretended to try and injure me again, but I managed to narrowly avoid the articulated lorry they sent to crush every bone in my body.

So being fit and healthy again and about to go off to the World Cup for a month, me and Vivian decided to throw a party. We thought it would be a great way to lift everyone's spirits and bring a sense of togetherness to the whole squad and indeed the whole nation.

Initially Viv wanted to actually invite everyone in the country, but even taking into account those who wouldn't have been able to make it, I reckoned that would be somewhere in the region of forty to forty-five million people, far too many for our tiny bedsit.

In the end we settled on squad members and their immediate families, which meant first cousins and in-laws, but not half-sisters or bisexual siblings. We also invited a few celebrities, such as Stan Boardman, Roy 'Chubby' Brown and the boys from Jethro Tull. And of course we invited Posh and Becks.

All in all it was a great night. The four of us who were able to make it, me, Viv, our left back's first cousin's wife and our reserve goalie's nephew, had a wild time; I even got an eight-letter word playing Boggle.

With the frivolities over, I became focused on the World Cup. It was taking place in Japansouthkorea, a country that was actually two countries somewhere far away. Our tactics were to try and win every game and not lose, a philosophy that Mr Vodaphone instilled in us using basic brainwashing techniques that anyone who's ever been involved with a cult will be familiar with.

To be honest, even though I'd been passed fit to play with crutches, I knew in my heart of heart of lungs that I wasn't one hundred per cent crutch match fit. I reckon it would have taken at least another four or five games on crutches to get me to that level, and those were four or five games we didn't have. Nonetheless, a captain is more about inspiring the team than actually being able to play, and I was certainly able to do that. Thanks to me we got through the group stage, then won our next game, before coming up against the mighty Brazil.

Brazil are the giants of world football. It's a religion over there. Everywhere you go there are huge statues of balls that you have to bow down to when you pass or be publicly whipped. Every day people gather outside the great Pelé's house and sacrifice goats and other grass-eating quadrupeds. It is considered a sin not to be able to dribble past four players and smack a banana shot into a goal. So we knew it was going to be tough.

From the start their fans kept up an incessant drumbeat on some drums and further distracted us by having two scantily clad women dancing provocatively in their midst. Nonetheless, at half time the score was one-all and we were still in the game.

'Come on, we can do this,' I said inspirationally as the lads ran out for the second half and I hobbled after them.

As the game progressed, though, I became less sure. I didn't say anything of course, but the Brazilians upped it a gear, from reverse to third, and I could see we were struggling. Then they won a free kick about forty yards out.

'Don't worry, lads,' I shouted even more inspirationally, 'it's too far out for them to try anything.'

But I hadn't counted on that Brazilian magic. As Ronaldmacdonaldinho stepped up to take the kick, one of the scantily clad dancing women appeared to lift her top up, revealing a firm breast and pert nipple. I hoped none of the other lads had seen it, but I hoped in vain. As the ball floated into our penalty area our goalie, Damien Sealion, was utterly transfixed by the display of bare, naked lady's bosom. His mind elsewhere, the ball simply looped over him and into the net.

The Brazilian lady in question claimed she'd meant to do

it, but the chances of a titty exposure beating a keeper of that stature are so remote, I believe it was a pure fluke.

As for me, I'd done everything I could on the inspirational front, I'd been inspirationally inspirational, so there was no way I could be blamed for anything that happened. No way.

The simple truth of the matter, though, was we were out of the World Cup, again.

Football wasn't going to be coming home.

We were.

Economy class on the six o'clock flight from Seoul airport. And there weren't even any window seats.

CHAPTER 11:

Wherefore art thou o King Lear?

'The Marshmallows you fucking idiot!'

I've always wanted a baby brother – someone to watch over, to teach, to batter. It was a bit of a joke in our family. Whenever Mum got in from work or the shops, I'd call out hopefully, 'Are you pregnant with a boy yet?' After a while, her negative responses to this query made me a bit despondent, so I shortened it to, 'Pregnant yet?' Dad wasn't too hot about this line of questioning – he felt it threatened both his masculinity and the hand-tool arrangements in his garden shed, so eventually I accepted the painful truth. Don't get me wrong – I love my sisters – but if a long-lost brother came along I'd readily swap them.

This childhood disappointment convinced me that *our* second child would be a girl. The gene pool indicated it, and a clairvoyant I consulted at a burger van in a lay-by off the M6 confirmed it. Even Chorlton-Cum-Hardy was ready-ing himself for a sister. He'd started to familiarise himself with areas he considered traditionally 'female', like perms, catfights and tampons. Vivian and I spent hours trying to choose a girl's name. I liked 'Pan Fresh', she rated 'Candy-floss'. After an amazing weekend in Holland, though, we finally settled on 'The Hague'.

I love Vivian when she's pregnant. As well as all the fun we had with her morning sickness – she also got all grouchy and irritable and kept saying things like 'Aaaaaaaaaaaaaaaaaaaaaaaaagggggghhhh.'

Towards the end, though, she felt bulky and uncomfortable and decided to do something about it.

'I'm going on a mini-tour, David,' she told me one night.

'We've already seen the hospital birth rooms,' I replied.

'No, David – I mean a mini *musical* tour – gigs, merchandise, that sort of thing.'

'You're nine months pregnant,' I said. 'What nightclub in England provides an epidural service with fully qualified anaesthetists to oversee it?'

She was stumped for a moment by my grasp of interventionist medical procedure, but hit back quickly.

'I will not be enslaved by my condition,' she shouted. 'I'm doing this in solidarity with all creative, pregnant wimmin.'

I was gearing up for a lengthy verbal joust but Viv quickly sealed my mouth with duct tape and ran out of the bedsit. I considered pursuing her, but I respected her independent thinking. Plus she'd taken the car, and the night buses round our way weren't very reliable. I peeled off the tape and sat on the bed for half an hour. I thought about her actions and nursed the chafed skin around my lips.

She returned in the early hours, clasping an A4 photocopy of her gig itinerary. I had to hand it to her. Getting a spot at the Stoat and Sebaceous Cyst was a bit of a coup. She was on a roll and I knew that to stand in her way would be folly. So, I spoke to Oona the babysitter about the possibility of some really long sessions. She was inside a grandfather clock at the time, but I think she heard me.

Vivian's tour took in ten dates and the first was at The Jovial Selection Box, near Macclesfield. She and her hastily assembled band would be getting a split of the door takings or a percentage of the casked ale sales.

Viv had made a few noises in the car on the way there and at one point I'd had to pull off on to a slip road while she sang 'Bohemian Rhapsody' at the top of her voice – including all one hundred and twenty vocal overdubs.

'Shouldn't we just go straight to the hospital?' I implored her.

'Scaramouche,' she answered.

The Jovial was pretty packed that night. It was a mixed crowd, mainly Anglican bishops and Glaswegian net curtain designers.

I knew from the first beat of the first bar of the first song that Vivian was in the latter stages of labour. Her vocals came out as agonising shrieks, as she writhed on the floor. She was less than a minute into the first number, when an enormous Hell's Angel named Death stormed on to the stage. I took cover under a pinball machine, sensing the imminence of a full-scale brawl. But Death looked out at the audience through the blinding stage lights and shouted: 'Has anyone got any warm towels?'

It turned out he was a senior midwife and team-leader at a local primary care centre. When a spotty young lad approached Death and asked for a refund because of the cancelled show, Death looked the kid up and down and hissed: 'You wanna see a show? Right, you're my assistant – hold these nasal tweezers.'

The kid was so shocked he quickly got stuck in. Death was incredible. For a man with such huge hands, his touch was tender and dextrous. At one stage he talked about using the Jovial's bathroom plunger for a Vantouse delivery, but it never came to that.

'It's another boy!' I cried out to Vivian, as Death gently held up the newborn infant. 'It's a brother for Chorlton-Cum-Hardy.'

The audience cheered ecstatically.

Vivian slapped me in the face.

'What was that for?' I asked indignantly.

'I've only gone and bought loads of dresses and pink outfits!' she wailed.

'So what?' I yelled in excitement. 'Anyone can wear anything. It doesn't matter what clothes you've got, it's what's inside you.'

Death looked at me with a newfound respect. 'Right on, man,' he nodded approvingly.

I'd always thought that the birth of our second child would be far less exciting than the first. But it was every bit as brilliant as when Chorlton-Cum-Hardy was born. I wept and wept as Vivian told me to get a grip and stood up to resume the musical number she'd interrupted.

'Sit down for fuck's sake!'

I turned, expecting Death to be issuing this stern command, but it was the zitty kid. He was loving his spot at the birthing table. I've heard he's a top surgeon now, or is it a wood-chip recycler?

Vivian calmed down and Death did the Apgar Test. He nodded with satisfaction.

'Everything's cool,' he smiled. 'You've got yourself a little beauty.'

The audience were screaming for an encore and another pregnant woman stage-dived to the front.

I hugged Death, but when acne kid went to hug me, I backed away quickly. Some of his juicier pimples looked like they were on the verge of exploding. I thanked everyone at the Jovial and made my way out, only stopping to put 10p in a fruit machine. As if the evening hadn't been amazing enough, I won the 50p jackpot and vowed to invest some of it in the boys' futures.

As I was helping Vivian into the car, Death ran out of the Jovial carrying something in a leather bag.

'I thought you might want this,' he smiled, handing it over. Inside was our baby, cooing ever so slightly.

'Whatever,' said Vivian, grabbing the bag.

'What are you going to call him?' asked Death.

'We were so convinced it was a girl that we haven't really thought much about boys' names,' I replied.

'I have,' said Vivian. 'I like King Lear.'

Death laughed and started to talk about his passion for Shakespeare. Vivian closed the window on his hand and ordered me to drive away.

We got back home and braced ourselves for the moment when Chorlton-Cum-Hardy would first meet his baby brother. When we went in, Oona put a finger to her lips. 'He's fast asleep,' she whispered, 'and he asked not to be woken until breakfast TV starts.'

The following morning, Chorlton-Cum-Hardy took to King Lear immediately. It was very moving to watch. And in the next few days, they bonded even more. By the end of the week, they were even co-operating together to make a more than passable Waldorf salad.

However, while I was ensconced in domestic bliss, things were going from bad to worse on the football front. My relationship with the gaffer was spinning out of control. He blanked me in the dressing room and whenever I tried to strike up a conversation, he'd cover his ears and sing: 'La la la la la la, I'm not listening.'

On other occasions I'd be having a chat with one of the lads, only to discover later that the boss had been behind my back all of the time, pulling faces at me and making lewd hand gestures. I'm a pretty thick-skinned type of guy, but I decided that enough was enough. I needed to confront him.

The perfect opportunity arose when I saw him at the supermarket one evening. He was strolling through the cereal aisle, humming to himself and scattering boxes of Shreddies on the floor. I hid behind the shelter of a giant Alpen pack, planning my approach. When I revealed myself, he looked at me sternly in the same way that a vet watches an animal that's about to be put down.

'What do you want?' he asked scornfully.

'I'm getting really bad vibes off you, boss,' I explained. 'I feel like you're shutting me out and I don't know why.'

He thought about this for a second and looked into my basket, shaking his head. 'You can get Shredded Wheat Bite Size far cheaper down the road,' he observed.

I made a quick note of this consumer information, but looked at him pleadingly, waiting for an answer to my original question.

'There's a problem, David,' he began. 'Recently I've begun to ask myself if you're really committed to the team. It seems that you want to spend an awful lot of time with your family and on spending sprees in Mothercare. Something's changed in you.'

'I'm totally committed to the team!' I stammered. 'You and the lads are my family.'

He didn't hear much of this retort, because he was busy studying the nutrition panel on the side of a pack of Golden Grahams.

'What was that?' he asked, pulling open a packet of Special K and crunching the contents with his left hand.

There was no way I was going to be talked to like that and I stormed out, forgetting my basket and sheepishly returning a minute later to reclaim it.

Our little 'chat' hadn't cleared the air at all. I was furious with him and he clearly despised me.

We had a game coming up that Sunday and I knew I'd only be able to get there twenty minutes before the kick-off. There was a sumo-wrestling bout at Chorlton-Cum-Hardy's school between the headmistress and a classroom assistant called Miss Compton. There was no way I was going to miss it. Chorlton-Cum-Hardy would be selling marshmallows during the half-time break. He'd be devastated if I wasn't there.

Of course I could have gone to the wrestling bout and not said anything to the gaffer about it. I could have told him I'd got stuck in traffic or had jury service or something to explain my tardiness. But I prided myself on being honest with him.

'How much are they?' he barked at me when I told him.

'How much are what?' I asked.

'The marshmallows, you fucking idiot!'

'It's fifty pence for three,' I told him.

'You can get them much cheaper down the road,' he sneered.

I wasn't prepared to stand around and have my son's pricing policy questioned. I walked away cursing him in as many languages as I could muster. We said no more about it, but I knew things weren't sorted.

The game in question was against Runcorn Raiders in the CND North West Challenge Cup. I was a sub. We were on form that day. Brevilley scored a brace, one of which he curled in from behind the clubhouse. In the eighty-eighth minute the gaffer sent me on for Miggsy. Thirty seconds later he took me off. I stormed over to the touchline.

'What the hell's going on?' I demanded.

The boss was clearly in a conciliatory mood.

'I'm the manager and I can do what I like. If you can't live with that, you can fuck off.'

And just to ram this point home he proceeded to send on two of the other subs, bring them off, put them on again and then bring one of them off again.

As I angrily hurried away from the pitch, Vivian jumped

out of a bush. She'd been using her metal detector to locate Roman hairpins in the area.

'What are you doing out here?' I asked.

'I paid Mr Ferfuson a visit this morning,' she said.

I shook my head in disbelief. My wife going to my boss? Why hadn't she done it sooner?

'He reckons you've got a bit flash. Says since you were made captain of the England team, you've been throwing your weight around, asking for two straws instead of one, down the pub, that sort of thing.'

I was stunned and the next day went to see him.

'Viv told me all about your little conversation,' I snapped. 'I can't believe you really think I've changed since Mr Vodaphone gave me the captain's armband. You're persecuting me.'

'I think persecution is too strong a word,' he said thoughtfully. 'I'm picking on you, giving you grief, making your life an absolute misery, but not persecuting you.'

I accepted this answer and thought that at last we were back on good terms.

The next club game was against Garston Academics, one of our great rivals. The boss was edgy before the game and completely freaked out when he discovered that our goalie, Steve, had suffered a shoulder injury when leading hunt the thimble at his daughter's eighteenth birthday party.

Mr Ferfuson stroked his chin for forty minutes, trying to find a solution. Eventually he looked up and said to me, 'You'll have to go in goal for this game, David.'

While some of the other lads started cursing in Aramaic, I grinned with pride. This would be my chance to show Mr Ferfuson how committed I really was. I'd dive, parry and intercept so brilliantly that he'd be on his knees to me by the end of the game.

Unfortunately things didn't quite go to plan. For a start,

Steve's gloves were enormous. I knew that he sometimes used them as sleeping bags.

During the game, I did loads of dives and jumps, but only when the ball was up the other end. When an opposing player finally hurtled towards me, I quickly got out a protractor to work out how to narrow the angle most efficiently. I was jotting down notes, when the ball flew into the net.

I held up my hands to show it wasn't my fault, but noticed out of the corner of my eye a raging Mr Ferfuson screaming at me from the bench and menacingly shaking his hardened knuckles.

They were two–nil up by half time. I was blameless for their second goal. It wasn't my fault that one of the Garston fans kept texting me and attaching photos of famous vets. He was a really interesting guy, but mysteriously the texts stopped coming after the ball had whistled into the top corner of our net.

Mr Ferfuson's team talk in the break was unbelievable. He was bubbling over with rage and for some reason vented his anger on me.

'Your performance was a disgrace,' he exploded. 'You let in two of the softest goals I've ever seen.'

'I was unsighted,' I said.

'Bollocks!'

'I was sighted,' I tried.

'THIS HAS GOT TO STOP!' he shouted. 'Take the blame for once.'

'But they weren't my fault!' I protested.

He had really lost it this time and stomped over to the far side of the changing room. On the floor were several parcels of food that Mr Ferfuson was meant to take to his grandma's house that night. He stood behind these victuals and lashed out with his foot.

As everyone sat watching in stunned silence, a medium-sized roast chicken and side dish of oven chips flew towards me and landed on my head, sliding down my front and depositing great swathes of fat and grease on my face and shirt. I looked anxiously over to Mr Ferfuson. Was there any dessert in that food bundle?

I was completely speechless. This was unacceptable. I made up my mind to visit our local library and appraise myself of the legal position viz à viz à viz à viz physical assault with a concealed poultry-based food item.

I tidied myself up and walked out, passing Mr Ferfuson by the door, who by now was hungrily tucking into some spinach filo pastry parcels.

As I left, I knew that things between us would never be the same.

When I got home, Vivian and the boys were tidying the flat: she was hoovering, Chorlton-Cum-Hardy was dusting and King Lear was putting the duvet cover through a mangle. I felt like a little kid going to their mum after being told off in school.

'Something stinks round here,' said Vivian as I walked in. I looked down at my grease-spattered shirt and took it off.

I began to tell Vivian about that afternoon's drama. She listed attentively.

'David, can you get out of the way, you're blocking the screen.'

She had sat down to watch an episode of *Kojak* dubbed into Icelandic. I put the boys to bed and sat down on the sofa next to Viv. She flicked the TV off and gave me one of her most serious looks. She reached down into her back pocket and pulled out a large piece of paper. She unfolded it. And unfolded it some more. And unfolded it even more. She had borrowed an origami book from the local library.

'What's that?' I asked.

'This is our latest bank statement,' she explained. 'Those are the outgoings,' she said, pointing to a gargantuan column of figures. 'And those represent income,' she added, indicating a column that read '£19.99'.

I was lost. High finance just wasn't my thing.

Vivian sighed. 'All right, let's put it another way. We're Bon Accord and we're losing 36–nil to Arbroath.'

I suddenly got it.

'Shit,' I said, 'you mean, we're losing heavily in the game of life?'

Vivian nodded.

'So what do you want me to do about it?' I asked.

Vivian sighed. 'How do most people get their hands on money, David?'

'Steal it?'

She shook her head.

'Forge it?'

She shook her head again.

'Find it?'

She shook her head a third time.

'No, David, they *earn* it. They go out and earn it.'

I didn't like where this conversation was going.

'What are you saying?' I asked her.

'You've got to get a job. And fast. We need a major injection of cash.'

I looked at her for a few seconds. 'Well why can't you earn the money?' I asked.

She laughed derisively. 'What, and give up singing? Don't be ridiculous.'

I knew this moment had been coming for a while but it still hurt. I was a footballer not a worker. Employment was just one meaningless step on the road to nowhere and I didn't want to go there. Even by cab.

But Vivian was deadly serious. Our finances were in a

mess. Drastic steps were required. I grabbed the phone and dialled a familiar number.

'Thank you for calling the offices of Teeny Weeny Mata Hari Uberagents to the Stars Ltd,' the voice said.

'This is David Feckham, I need a job.'

'All our lines are busy right now,' said the voice.

I was so impressed with the consistency of their staff's phone patter.

'I'll work for anyone so long as they have a football team.'

'But if you'd care to leave a message someone will definitely get back to you as soon as humanly possible. Beep.'

'It's pretty urgent,' I explained. 'I'll wait by the phone for news.'

I waited by the phone, but it never rang. That's part of the deal when you're with a top agency. You're so important to them that sometimes they're a bit overawed by you – they feel shy or nervous about getting back to you.

Vivian found me asleep on the floor the next morning, cradling the phone. She waved a magazine in my face.

I sat up and studied it. *Booze Weekly*. There I was on the front cover – a great big mugshot of me in the dressing room yesterday, with the chicken and chips sliding down my front. It was pretty obvious that Mr Ferfuson had taken the photo. He often filmed people, with a camera he secreted in his bag. A couple of years ago he'd won a Bafta for his documentary on political resistance in the Trafalgar Square pigeon community.

Vivian was seething. 'We need to get out of this country,' she said. 'The press could easily destroy us. We need to move quickly and to do that we need you to find work.'

I was still admiring the photo and only looked up when she flicked my ear.

DAVID FECKHAM; MY BACKSIDE

'Who do we know who's got a proper job?'

We looked at each other, and at the same time, both of us said, 'Spike!'

I rang him immediately. He said that we shouldn't meet in the pub for obvious reasons. They weren't obvious to me, but he was calling the shots. He asked me to meet him in a hotel, in town.

When I got there at the appointed time, Spike was striding round the hotel lobby, wearing two suits and speaking on four mobile phones simultaneously. He looked completely different to the Neanderthal landlord I knew so well. As soon as he clocked me, he flipped them all shut.

'David,' he said, walking over and grasping my hand firmly.

'Spike,' I responded.

'Call me Stuart here,' he whispered.

We sat down at a small table and he ordered some petit-fours.

'Listen, David, I'll cut to the chase,' he began. 'I know of two openings at the moment – both related to timeshare properties – one in Greece, one in Spain.'

I listened attentively, making a small Elizabethan sculpture on the table in front of us with some sugar cubes.

'The Greek one would mean Vivian could play the cruise ships,' he continued. 'There's a lot of money in that game if you know your port from your starboard. And there's definitely a chance for her to do some of what we loosely refer to as "modelling" work.'

'Does the Greek outfit have a football team?' I asked.

Spike made a call on each of his mobiles and shook his head.

'No they don't,' he informed me. 'But they do have a semi-pro curling side.'

I shook my head. 'No way.'

'Just give me a minute,' he said, pulling out another two mobiles and making six more calls.

His face suddenly creased into a smile.

'The Spanish company *does* have a football team,' he beamed. 'Apparently they play in the West Costa del Sol League Division 6 (South).'

I punched the air in delight.

'What do I have to do?' I asked.

He pulled out a single sheet of paper and crossed the two places I needed to sign.

'Welcome on board,' he said with a wide grin. 'You start in two weeks. There's a tiny basic salary but a very generous commission package, if you sell a hundred units a day.'

I shook his hand.

On one level I was absolutely gutted. The thought of doing a decent day's work filled me with dread.

But on the plus side, I'd be playing in Europe. La Liga was arguably the best domestic league on the continent.

After 13 years in which I'd been Schnitzel and Parrot through and through I was off.

I couldn't wait to get home and tell Vivian and the boys.

This year, we were off to sunny Spain.

E viva España.

CHAPTER 12:

Going, going gone (sold to the Spanish gentleman in the sombrero)

'Group hug.'

Those first few days after the decision to leave Manchester had been taken were odd to say the least. The weather was unseasonally sub-tropical and the city was hit by a plague of locust. A volcano erupted in Piccadilly bus station and a series of lightning strikes by tilers led to a shortage of grout, the ramifications of which are still being felt today. Elsewhere, though, it was business as usual.

The Schnitzel and Parrot had three more games left to play in the season and I was determined to honour my contract with them, even though I didn't actually have a contract. But things being at rock bottom with Mr Ferfuson I wasn't sure if I'd even get on the bench, let alone in the starting line-up.

Since the 'chicken' incident all semblance of cordiality had broken down between us. On three occasions he'd attacked me with a pair of secateurs and he'd once donned full body armour, mounted a horse and come at me with a twenty-foot jousting pole. Nonetheless I was confident that professionalism would win through at the end of the day and he'd put the team's needs before any petty squabble.

He knew about my move to Spain of course, as did everyone else. It hadn't really come as much of a shock to those who were close to me and knew what had been going on. To a certain extent it was even a relief. Not to say that me and the gaffer hadn't tried to patch things up – we had. But after our sessions at Relate had failed to sort things out it was obvious that the end was nigh. It was just a matter of when. And where. And how. And if.

I'd left the details of the move to Spain to my agents. I knew they'd sort me out a good deal; that's the beauty of having agents, they take the weight of things like that off your shoulders, and every other part of your body, so that you can concentrate on doing what you do best: playing football, if you're a footballer.

So I was in a pretty relaxed frame of mind when I entered the Schnitzel and Parrot to find out if I'd be playing that Sunday.

'Hola señor,' said Brevilley as I sat down at the beer, crisp and semolina-strewn table.

Ever since I'd signed for the Spaniards, Brevilley had been saying that to me – I had absolutely no idea why.

'All right,' I said. 'Is the team sheet up for Sunday?'

'Oh yes, si si,' he said.

I'd gone easy on the blusher that day so I had no idea why he was calling me a sissy, but I let it go; I knew better than to mess with Brevilley when he was being a twat.

I approached the corkboard on which the team sheet was pinned with no little trepidation. I felt like a condemned man making his last walk before being executed in the electric chair or by lethal injection or by hanging from the neck until I was dead. I turned to look at the faces of my friends; they all seemed to be pointing at me and laughing. I knew it was just my imagination playing tricks, but it felt so real.

I reached the board and scanned the sheet of A4 paper

that was hanging loosely from it. Or maybe it was A3. I couldn't tell or care.

There was no sign of my name in the starting line-up. Nor amongst the subs, though one of them, Chad Mavikdef, was an anagram of my name; a somewhat cruel and, in my opinion, unnecessary trick that fate had played on me. (And, to an extent, Mr Ferfuson as he'd forced the lad to change his name by deed poll.)

I was about to turn and walk away, when something caught my eye at the bottom of the page. Perhaps it was A2, who knows? I looked again just to be sure. Yes, there it was. In black and white. And yellow and green crayon. Ball boy: David Feckham. My heart missed a beat and I made a mental note to book an appointment with a cardiologist. I'd been right about Mr Ferfuson. When push had come to shove, as it most certainly had, he'd been totally professional. I felt the sting of salty tears well up in my eyes, and in my ears. I staggered over to the bar in a daze.

'I, I, I'm going to be there, I'm on the team sheet,' I said to Spike, who had now reverted from 'Stuart' to his normal persona.

'Pleased to hear it, Fecks,' he said, with just the slightest sense that he was overplaying 'this' personality. 'And by the way, there's something else. We were going to tell you later, but I don't see why we can't tell you now.'

I had no idea who the 'we' he was referring to was – no one else was talking. It crossed my mind that he meant him and Stuart, but that thought scared me too much so I let it go.

'We've organised a testimonial for you. The Schnitzel and Parrot versus Fun in the Sun Timeshare Apartments Ltd XI.'

He paused for a moment to let the full effect of what he'd just said sink in. It didn't so he made it blindingly obvious.

'They're the team you're going to be playing for in Spain

– the one that that other geezer who I don't know sorted out for you.'

That hit home. I couldn't believe it. A testimonial. For me! I was so happy, I kissed everyone in the pub, one or two with tongues, and walked home on cloud two.

Mr Ferfuson remained professional through to the end of the season. I was ball boy for all of the last three games, and played no small part in the team winning them all. As the final whistle of my final league game blew I felt a slight constriction in my throat. To most people our ground was just a field, a few sods in the middle of nowhere. But to me it was a theatre of dreams. It held so many memories, many of which I couldn't remember; leaving it would be like leaving a part of me behind. That felt almost impossible to do, but the company I contacted about having the turf transported out to Spain had given us an astronomical quote for the job, so behind it would have to be left.

As a final tribute the lads hoofed the ball as far away from the pitch as they could and let me go get it one last time. Then we all headed to the pub for a last post-match drink – apart from the one we'd be having after the testimonial.

'Now, you're sure you've got the tickets and everything,' said Vivian when I returned home later that night.

'It's all sorted, babe,' I slurred, somewhat the worse for wear. Uncle Cedric had insisted I match him pint for pint. It wasn't easy. I felt like Cool Hand Fecks. But I did it. And now the blood pumping through my veins was pure alcohol.

'My agents are taking care of it,' I managed to splutter before collapsing to the ground, destroying an original 1970s lava lamp in the process.

The following day we were due to fly out from Manchester airport on the 12.15 to Malaga. Given that we'd have to be at the airport two hours beforehand and it was a 45-

minute drive to the airport, my testimonial had been arranged to kick off at seven in the morning. It was an awkward time, but then I'd watched matches played during the last World Cup in Japansouthkorea kick off at that time, so I knew it wouldn't be a problem. All I needed now was some beauty kip to ensure I was on top form the following day.

I awoke at five-thirty a.m. My customary waking piss was pure John Smiths. That, coupled with the fact that King Lear had been up half the night with chronic colic (try saying that after a skinful!), meant I wasn't exactly feeling my best. It didn't worry me though; even at fifty per cent I was nine per cent better than everyone else on the pitch put together. I showered and changed into my kit.

'I'll see you at the airport,' I said to Vivian as I kissed one of the bags under her eyes.

I drove the familiar route to the pitch feeling as if my life was at a crossroads. Ahead was Spain. To the left was a Tesco superstore, and to the right, a safari park. I knew I had to go straight on, though the safari park was tempting.

It was six-fifteen when I pulled into the car park at the ground. I'd only got lost three times en route, a personal best for me, and thus had plenty of time to prepare mentally, physically, spiritually and endocrinologically for the game.

The other lads arrived soon after. If they were feeling highly emotional due to my imminent departure they hid it well. A couple, Miggsy and Scooby, disappeared off somewhere, possibly to shed a private tear, or maybe to do 'swaps' for their Panini sticker albums. But most of them went about their pre-match routines as if it was 'just another game'.

Then Mr Ferfuson entered the changing room. I instantly felt his eyes pierce into me, though it could have been a stanley knife. The love that had been lost between us was destined to remain forever unfound.

'Right, listen up,' he said, the timbre of his voice resonating in my every pore. 'This lot are bound to fancy themselves a bit, but remember, they're foreign, so they won't like it up 'em, which means that's exactly what we're going to do to them, got it?'

Everyone nodded in unison and then one after the other in a sort of Mexican-wave nod. Mr Ferfuson then proceeded to read out the starting line-up. If I was being honest I'd have to say I had wondered how he would deal with me, though if I was being dishonest I'd say I wanted to kiss his balding pate.

Understandably he'd gone for the same starting eleven that had done so well in those last three games of the season, but then I got the shock of my life.

'Okay, subs,' he said. 'Sleepy, Dopey, Fatty, Skinny, the Aga Khan and Fecks.'

At first I couldn't believe it. Had the boss actually said my name? I had to be sure.

'B-B-Boss,' I stammered.

'Y-Y-Yes,' he said, also stammering for some reason.

'Did you say, "Fecks"?'

He checked down his list.

'Why yes, I believe I did.'

I still couldn't believe it.

'B-B-Boss,' I stammered again.

'Y-Y-Yes,' he stammered back again.

'Did you say, "Why yes, I believe I did"?'

He checked his memory banks.

'Why yes, I believe I did,' he said.

This time there was no doubting it. My heart did a little jump for joy as I pulled on my jockstrap. I followed the other lads out on to the pitch, the dawn sun hitting me in the face as I stepped out of the tunnel and into the dawn sun. It was like a waking dream, or a dreaming reality.

'Oi, Fecks.'

I started, jolted out of my reverie by the loud, throaty voice. Looking up I saw it was Spike.

'Hello,' I said, 'what are you doing here?' He wasn't a big footy fan, Spike, preferring the gentler attractions of kabaddi.

'I came to give you this,' he said, handing me a crisp five-pound note.

'What . . .' I began, but he was way ahead of me.

'I sold three tickets for this game making a total of £3.78. After a meeting of the pub finance committee we decided to round it up to a fiver.'

My gob was well and truly smacked this time. When you witness human kindness on such a scale it takes your breath away. I didn't know what to say.

'No need to say anything, mate,' said Spike, 'just get out there and score a few tries.' As I said, football wasn't really Spike's game, but I knew what he meant.

I joined the rest of the lads for the pre-match warm-up. As I started on my squat thrusts I glanced over at my team-mates-to-be, warming up in the other half. It was odd to think that very soon I'd be playing alongside them, that they'd be my mates and we'd go round to each other's houses for games of cribbage and Sleeping Lions.

On this occasion, though, they were the enemy and I was determined to cut them no slack. And just in case they were in any doubt as to where my loyalties lay, as I walked over to take my seat on the subs' bench, I elbowed their centre half in the face.

As the first half kicked off I looked over at the gaffer, hoping beyond hope to catch his eye. I knew the game was only a few seconds old, but already I reckoned Puttsy was having a 'mare and deserved to be pulled off. I was right about Puttsy, who wasn't happy about being substituted after only eleven seconds, but sadly it was Skinny who got the nod from Mr Ferfuson.

By half time we were one up and had used two more subs. Midway through the second half we went two up and the gaffer decided to tighten things up in defence by throwing Dopey into the fray. That left just me and the Aga Khan on the bench.

With five minutes to go we were still two up and heading for a well-deserved victory.

'Khany,' said the gaffer, 'get stripped off. You're going on.'

I looked at the boss as he said those words, studying his every facial expression in the hope that I'd find one that said, *and you're going on next, Fecks*. But all I found was a look that I took to mean, *I hope it's chicken tonight.*

It seemed as if I'd played my last game for The Schnitzel and Parrot, but then, just as had happened so many times in the past, fate entered from stage left. I heard what sounded like the theme tune from *Black Beauty*.

'What's that?' I said.

'Ach, it's my mobile,' said the Aga Khan.

He bent down to pick it up from his bag.

'Yes. I see. When? Are you sure? Are you sure sure? Okay, I'll be there as soon as I can.' He sighed. 'Boss,' he said, 'one of my horses has developed a bad case of equine laryngitis. I have to go.'

Mr Ferfuson remained impassive. As the Aga Khan walked away the full extent of the gulf that had opened up between us become obvious. He was simply unable to bring himself to even speak to me at this point. Instead, using Makaton sign language for the deaf, he signed, 'Fecks, you're on.'

I was stripped and ready for action in no time at all.

'Thanks, boss,' I said, 'you know I won't let you down.'

Within moments I was right in the thick of the action. My first task was to help defend a corner. Positioning myself on the edge of our six-yard box, as the ball came in I decided to play it flash; it was my last game for the pub, I reckoned it was all right to showboat a little. I went for an overhead kick and connected perfectly. Unfortunately somewhere in the air my sense of spatial awareness went haywire and what should have been a great clearance became a great shot at goal, and one that our keeper was unable to save.

A minute later, the Spanish side got a free kick and floated another cross into our box. This time I went for a diving header. Once again I connected perfectly, but once again my positioning let me down and the ball ended up in our net.

Buoyed by their comeback, the Fun in the Sun team launched one last attack. As their forward dribbled into our penalty area I went to tackle him. I connected perfectly with the ball, but, according to the ref, caught him in the shin, thigh and neck first. He pointed to the spot.

A central midfielder stepped up to take the kick. He hit it low and hard to his right, but our goalie guessed correctly and made a brilliant save. I ran to congratulate him, unaware, in my ecstasy, that the ball was still in play. I booted it with my left foot and it curled over our spread-eagled keeper, off an upright and into the net.

Seconds later the ref blew the final whistle. We had lost three–two and I had scored a hat-trick of own goals. You couldn't write stuff like that. Personally I was overjoyed. Okay they were own goals, but they were still goals, and cracking ones at that. I looked heavenward and gave the big guy a little wink.

I couldn't hang around after the game, which was fine by

me. I hate goodbyes, I'm much better with hellos and 'wotchers', so I took one last, longing look at the pitch and the lads, and then I was off to the airport and my new life.

It was only nine-thirty when I got there, but, even though it had already been the most amazing day, more twists and turns than a corkscrew still lay ahead.

I found Viv and the boys tucking into a McDonald's breakfast. The boys were Mchaving a Mcboiled Mcegg and Mcsoldiers, whilst Viv was having a Mccup of Mctea and a helping of Mcblack Mcpudding.

'All right,' she said, 'you got the tickets then?'

'Has no one from the agency showed?' I asked.

'No. The only person who's approached us was a Norwegian guy from Jews for Jesus asking if we'd like to go to a meeting.'

'What did you say?' I asked.

'I said I felt the whole notion of Jews thinking Jesus is the messiah is very odd, and asked him why they don't just become Christians?'

'What did he say?'

'He said I was right and went off to convert.'

'Good work,' I said. 'Now, don't worry, I'm sure one of my agents will turn up with the tickets soon.'

Four Mcpeppermint Mcteas and a Mcsparkling Mcwater later I was not so sure.

'You did tell them exactly what we were doing, didn't you, David?' said Viv.

'Well not exactly, but they've got their noses to the ground, they'll know what's going on,' I said.

But I wasn't so sure. The world I inhabit is full of rumour and counter-rumour. Incredible as it may seem, completely untrue stories are sometimes passed off as fact just so that someone can garner a little publicity. It occurred to me that maybe they'd assumed my going to Spain was just such a story, perhaps put about to increase my transfer value. I was just sensing the beginnings of a major panic attack when over the tannoy I heard: 'Could Mr Feckham come to the meeting point on level four?'

'See,' I said, exhaling great gasps of hot relief. 'Come on.'

Viv downed the last of her Mcwhateveritwasshewasdrinking and scooped up a boy in each arm. Five minutes later we were approaching the meeting point, expecting someone from my agency to be waiting with our tickets. But when we saw who was there, we couldn't believe our eyes.

'All right, Davey boy, long time no see.'

It was Uncle Terry. And with him were Mum, Dad, Katie and Clare.

'I'm scared,' said Chorlton-Cum-Hardy, siphoning himself off behind Viv's legs.

I laughed: the thought of anyone being scared of my family was ridiculous, especially at this particular moment when the love flowing between us was obvious for all to see.

'Oh Chorlton-Cum-Hardy,' I said, 'there's nothing to be scared of.'

'Yes there is,' he exclaimed from the sanctuary of Viv's legs, 'that big ugly man's got a big knife.'

I laughed again, but then caught sight of a large serrated blade protruding from Uncle Terry's jacket. It seemed to have a few droplets of blood on it.

'Ha, ha,' laughed Uncle Terry, 'the youngster obviously doesn't know that I've taken up knife-throwing. And if you want to,' he continued, kneeling down and directing his words to Chorlton-Cum-Hardy, 'you can help me with my act – it'd be a pleasure to carve you up like the little slag you are.'

'There, you see, Chorlton-Cum-Hardy,' I interjected, 'it's just as I said, nothing to be scared of.'

Chorlton-Cum-Hardy looked at me and then threw up down the back of Viv's trousers.

'It's terrific to see you all,' I said as Viv and the boys headed off to find the nearest public convenience. 'I'm really touched that you've come to see me off. Mum, Dad, Katie, Clare. How have you been?'

'All right,' said Dad on behalf of all of them.

'Yeah, we're all great. Now listen, Davey my lad, we've got some, erm, presents for you.' It was Uncle Terry again. The man's kindness was overwhelming.

'I don't know what to say. Shall I open them now?'

'No, you fucking fuckwitted fuckwit,' shouted Uncle Terry, startling a party of Bhutanese schoolchildren nearby. 'They're not for you, they're for our friends in Spain. Someone will collect them off you when you get there, okay?'

Once again I'd underestimated the man. He was always thinking of others. My family had come to see me off – that was present enough for me.

Terry and the others then handed me all their presents. They were wrapped pretty conservatively in brown paper, but knowing them, I reckoned they'd saved on the paper so that they'd be able to spend more on the actual presents.

'No problem, Uncle Terry,' I said, 'I'll see to it that your pals get their gifts. There's just one thing though: I was expecting my agent to be here with the plane tickets, but there's been some mix-up and they haven't turned up.'

Terry raised his eyes in a playful, *doh, you silly sausage* type gesture. 'Leave it to me,' he said.

Five minutes later he was back with four plane tickets, and good ones at that, printed on strong, solid paper. It also seemed as if his blade had some more blood on it and I wondered if he'd performed his knife-throwing act to raise the money for the tickets, but I knew better than to ask.

I waved the tickets at Viv and the boys as they returned from the public convenience. The last cog in the wheel had fallen into place. We were going. All that was left was to say goodbye to my family.

'Group hug!' I shouted and marched towards them all, arms akimbo. 'Mmm, mmm, mmm,' I hummed as I felt their warm embrace. It was great, but something seemed a little odd; not least the fact that there were an awful lot more people in the group hug than there should have been. I opened my eyes. In front of me were thirty Bhutanese schoolchildren and their bemused teacher. It seemed that, unbeknownst to me, my family had manoeuvred them into my hug, and legged it themselves. I smiled. Jokers to the last.

As the plane took off I looked out of the window at the receding landscape. It was as if my entire life up to now was receding with it. Many thoughts were traversing my mind, foremost of which was whether, when asked at check-in if anyone had given us anything to take with us, we should have mentioned the gifts from my family, but I doubted there was much duty to pay on the various knick-knacks they almost certainly were, so decided to stop fretting about it.

Before long the seat-belt sign went off. I considered calling a stewardess over and telling her that it was faulty, but then I realised that everyone else's seat-belt sign had also gone off, so they probably knew about it already.

I got up to stretch my legs. I walked down the aisle and before I knew it found myself in the first-class area. I'd never flown first class before and was casually browsing the extensive range of potpourri available when I spotted the unmistakable hair of an old friend.

'David?' I said. 'David Beckham?'

He looked up, the twin pigtails he was currently sporting in his hair swaying gently as he did so.

'It's me, David Feckham. You know, we first met at that tournament in Manchester years ago and we've bumped into each other on the footy scene once or twice since then.'

He studied my visage.

'Of course I remember,' said Becks, 'and just like we agreed at that tournament, I've looked out for you.'

This was too much. I really could not believe what I was hearing.

'When you scored that goal against Dynamo Dollis Hill? I was there. When you played your first game for the Schnitzel and Parrot junior team? I was there. When you scored that incredible own goal for the senior team? I was there. When you got sent off against Argentina in the Pub Sunday League World Cup? I was there. When you were made captain of the England Pub Sunday League team? I was there. When Mr Ferfuson kicked a chicken and side dish of oven chips over you? I was there. And this morning? When you scored that incredible hat-trick of own goals in your testimonial?'

'Don't tell me,' I said. 'You were there.'

'Yeah,' he said.

He paused for a second and looked at me with a glow of empathy and support.

'And you know what?'

I shook my head, revelling in the moment.

'Your dad was right. You're rubbish.'

EPILOGUE

There's been an awful lot of water under the bridge since I ghost-wrote those first twelve chapters. As I sit here now with the ghost writers, Ivor 'Lofty' Baddiel and Johnny 'Ex-Eastender' Zucker, I'm finding it hard to assimilate everything that's happened in the last year, so that they can then go away and make it more interesting, funnier and less true.

The main thing I want to get across is this: for all the mud-slinging that's taken place – and believe you me there's been more mud slung since I left England than at that Glastonbury where it really rained a lot – I'm still fundamentally me; David Feckham, footballer, husband, father, timeshare apartment seller.

After our initial week in Spain, Viv and the boys returned to England. I could understand why: a week's a long time in politics, it's even longer in football, often running to nine, even ten, days. And the breakfast cereal portions out here are far smaller than even in the multi-pack boxes back home. The main reason though was Viv's career. She felt she was on the verge of cracking the English market. It was just a matter of being in the right place at the right time – that little bit of luck that people with no talent need to break through. In her opinion 2003 was definitely the right time, but Spain was not the right place. So off she went, taking the boys with her.

I was sad after I'd waved them off at the airport, because they meant everything to me, but I was also ecstatic as it meant I could concentrate 100% on my football (and 3% on selling timeshare apartments).

The first matter to be dealt with was adapting to the Continental game. This is something that lay people and those not involved in the game don't fully understand. They tend to think that a South American player coming to play in the Premiership could slot in as easily as a book being carefully replaced on a neat library shelf. Or that a player from Japan's J league could turn out for the US Olympic ladies' team as if he's been playing for them all his life. But it's just not that simple. Different countries' games have their own very subtle nuances and variations, often undetectable to the naked eye and indeed the naked flame, but there nonetheless. Getting used to them takes time, a lot of time, and a good manager will be prepared to spend that time schooling a new player in the ways of his new league. Ian Squint was just such a manager.

Ian was old school in everything but name. He took me to one side after my first training session with the Fun in the Sun Timeshare Apartments Ltd XI.

'I like what I see, Davy boy,' he said to me.

I followed his eyeline. He was looking at a replica of the Venus de Milo made out of beeswax. It was beautiful.

'How did you find it today?' he went on, his huge frame rattling with every syllable.

'Yeah good Ian, good, you do a few things different to what I'm used to but . . .'

'Exactly!' he blurted out, interrupting me with his inter-ruption. 'That's why from tomorrow I want you at our special training camp for foreign players who need to adapt to the Spanish game.'

'I'm not foreign,' I protested.

'You are out here, Davy boy,' he countered, and with that

he shuffled off laughing in that appallingly unsavoury way of his that I described in the introduction.

The regime at the training camp for foreign players who need to adapt to the Spanish game was tough. There were some English lads who'd been in there for years because they hadn't managed to modify their skills. I was determined not to be one of them, and dedicated myself to playing football the Spanish way. We had classes in How To Quell The British Instinct To Play The Long Ball Upfield, How To Wear A Hairband, How To Swear At The Ref In Spanish and How To Waste An Awful Lot Of Time. There were also heat and altitude classes. The camp had specially made indoor arenas where the temperature was kept at a constant 40 degrees centigrade. It was hell just standing in them, let alone running around for ninety minutes and extra time, but I didn't care; this was one kitchen I could stand the heat in and wasn't going to get out of.

I'm not going to pretend it was easy: it wasn't. But my target was to be ready to play for the first team by the time of the big derby against Bar Selona, a tapas establishment just outside Torremolinos. So when Ian came up to me two days before the game and said, 'You're ready, I need you for the game against Bar Selona,' I knew I was ready.

To say I was thrown in at the deep end would not be an understatement, it would be exactly right. I felt like Daniel in the lions' den or Russell Crowe in that scene from *Gladiator* – the one where he's thrown into the ring to fight some tigers, not the one where he's dead and sees his wife and child again. Running out of the makeshift tunnel – in actual fact an adapted windsock – the hatred and venom present was palpable; and that was just from my teammates towards me. The game itself was of no significance. We were both languishing in mid-table with no fear of promotion, relegation or spiders, but you'd never have known that from the way the players went at it. Tackles were flying in from everywhere, often arriving three or four minutes late. It really was like a bubbling cauldron in there, and one being stirred by some particularly unpleasant witches.

The game hinged on an incident deep into the 49 minutes of injury time that the ref had added on at the end of the first half. I'd been pleased with my performance, for a debut it hadn't been half-bad at all. I felt I'd managed to merge the old with the new to play a kind of Spenglish style of game. I also reckoned I'd formed the beginnings of quite a decent partnership with Sid Sidane, our centre forward, so when he picked up the ball 47 minutes into the injury time period I felt certain he'd pass to me. In fact I'm sure he thought about it as he looked up, but then his eyes focused on someone in the four-strong crowd behind me and he was off.

'Oy, Sid mate!' I shouted. 'What're you doing?'

'I've spotted a fresh punter, if I can get a sale out of her, I'll be up for a bonus this month,' he replied.

At first I didn't have a clue what he was on about, but as the other 'commission only' boys in the team started flocking towards a woman in the crowd, it all became clear.

Of course, with half our team off trying to flog a time-share apartment, Bar Selona were able to piss all over us. And that's exactly what they did. By the time Sid and the others had returned, having sold the woman a condo overlooking the harbour, complete with bone china bidet and a nest of hummingbirds, we were four down and the game was over.

It was a fiery introduction to Spanish football, but one that stood me in good stead for what lay ahead, which was more matches. With every one I felt my game becoming sharper and more suited to the league I was now playing in.

I was also a big hit with the fans, or fan to be exact: Mad Miguel. He followed us everywhere, and eventually started following me everywhere, so much so that I had to get a restraining order.

Off the pitch I also felt settled. I was living in a converted bullring just outside Malaga and spoke to Viv, Chorlton-Cum-Hardy and King Lear in my head as often as I could, and once or twice for real on the phone. All in all, life was pretty good. But then it went horribly wrong.

I don't want to harp on too much about 'IT' cos 'IT's all been very well documented, but 'IT' definitely had an effect on my game. Personally I didn't want to dignify 'IT' by giving 'IT' any more space in this book, but the publishers said, 'Forget your principles, just think of the sales,' and I knew they were right. So here in this very tome, I'm going to deal with all of the accusations connected to 'IT'. Below I list each one, accompanied by my bona fide rebuttal.

LIE: 'IT' began in a nightclub.
TRUTH: I'm barred from every nightclub on the Costa and Gibraltar. (I can get into clubs on Ibiza, but I have to wear spandex – Rave on!)

LIE: 'IT' involved sexual text messaging.
TRUTH: I don't even own a phone that has a sexual text messaging button function capability.

LIE: 'IT' all went on in plush hotel rooms.
TRUTH: I've never stayed anywhere with more than one star.

LIE: 'IT' led to me getting a wart on a certain part of my body.
TRUTH: I didn't. And even if I had, I could have treated it

immediately – I always carry a small flagon of liquid nitrogen.

LIE: 'IT' was a figment of my imagination.
TRUTH: Footballers have no imagination.

LIE: 'IT' involved three Spanish donkeys, a ramekin of pistachio nuts and a glockenspiel.
TRUTH: They were almonds.

Despite the fact that all of these rebuttals were published in our local rag, *La Sultana*, 'IT' still wouldn't go away. To be honest, there were times when I found 'IT' very difficult, but throughout 'IT' all, what kept me going during the darkest hours (predominantly those that took place at night) was the support I got from family and friends. Knowing they all believed me meant an awful lot.

I was overwhelmed by a postcard of solidarity I received, signed by my parents, my sisters, Uncles Terry and Cedric, Aunt Delia, everyone at The Schnitzel and Parrot, my agents, Miggsy and the lads and several local government ombudsmen. It arrived one rainy morning. The sudden downpour had smudged all the signatures to such an extent that they were practically unreadable, but I would recognise Spike's ink and calligraphy style anywhere, and knew what he'd done for me. (After all, he'd arranged my testimonial *and* donated the extra money.)

Viv and the boys were the last people to hear about 'IT'. She phoned me on a sultry, balmy, overcast night.

'David, I've just been reading this week's *La Sultana*,' she whinnied down the phone at me.

'I have too,' I replied. 'Wasn't Señorita Jamelia Olivera's tortilla recipe great: so simple to make, but delicious nonetheless.'

'David,' she whispered at the top of her voice. 'I'm talking about IT.'

'Oh,' I ejaculated.

'Is IT true?' she asked.

'Is what true?' I was playing for time. And with fire. And a game of Rummikub.

'That's all you need to say,' she rejoined. 'You've answered my question. I never believed IT for a second. Now we have to release the photos.'

I was confused. I hadn't answered her question, I'd been playing for time (and with fire and Rummikub). And what photos was she on about?

I didn't have to wait long to find out. In the following week's edition of *La Sultana* were a couple of photos of Hadrian's wall (obviously not the whole wall but a sizeable section of it). They spoke volumes. Not to me. But Vivian seemed chuffed with them.

It wasn't an easy time for the Feckham family, but as far as we were concerned the photos were there for all to see, so that should have been the end of IT.

(Incidentally, as if 'IT' wasn't enough, around the same time I had an affair. It happens in a lot of marriages and Viv was cool about it.)

Unfortunately, 'IT' wouldn't go away and I instructed a team of highly trained Beefeaters to look in to 'IT' for me – I'm still awaiting their report. 'IT' definitely affected me, though, and however much my yoga teacher pushed me, for the rest of the season, my performances were below par – excellent, but below par.

By the end of the season a distraction was at hand in the form of Pub Euro 2004 in Portugal. And it wasn't just the matches that excited me. I was relishing the prospect of trying out my recently acquired Spanish on the Portuguese.

With hindsight, certain people say I wasn't ready for the

tournament. Some claim that things off the pitch interfered with my preparations, but I say to them, there's no way I'd let assistant referees or advertising hoardings distract me in any way. Others insist I wasn't match fit and I want to put that little lie straight here. The reason I didn't go haring all over the pitch during the games was because a) I was conserving energy, and b) I was practising my speed walking for the Bruce Forsyth annual charity walkathon in Torquay.

As soon as the squad got together I got a really good feeling, and I wasn't alone. We all felt that this time we could really do something, even if it wasn't football related. Maybe we could lay some mosaic earthenware tiles, or win a Bananarama soundalike contest.

Even though I was totally confident about my place in the set-up, Mr Vodaphone assured me that I was still captain and the main man.

'You crisps toilet duck meander,' he told me during our first training session. OK, I was the only player taking part – the others had made comfortable nettle beds in the shade of an awning at the side of the pitch and were snoring loudly – but I could tell it was from his heart.

During those pre-tournament days, one thing became very clear. We had a new pretender in our midst. At eighteen Shane Spooney had the physique and mentality of a nineteen-year-old. Nothing seemed to faze the lad. If he came up against a brick wall, he just ploughed through it. I suppose being a hod carrier helped him in this respect, but he had so many other facets to his game. And he wasn't intimidated by my aura. He pushed me out of the way in the lunch queue just like the other lads. I loved this lack of deference wrapped up in big time respect.

By the time the tournament arrived, we were at our optimum strength and everyone was totally fired up. I even caught Mr Vodaphone performing some country dancing steps beside the hotel litter-bins.

Our first game, against France, was a travesty of justice. We scored near the start and held onto this slim lead until the 90th minute. When we heard a shrill whistling sound, our team took it to be the final whistle and started trooping off the pitch. Turns out it was one of those very high-pitched dog whistles which had been untuned and thus became audible to the human ear. Since the French players took no notice of it, we concluded that the fact it was blown by their manager was suspicious.

As we reached the dugout, we turned in horror to see the French scoring a goal, and before we could get back into positions, they were awarded a penalty and scored. We tried everything to make the referee change his mind, including offering to do up his holiday flat in Sardinia, but he wasn't having it.

The second match was against the Swiss, and we cruised it. They looked tough, but were easy to break down. At three–nil we started playing exhibition football. Mr Voda-phone took on the role of curator, whilst me and some of the lads filled out a series of complex application forms for national lottery funding.

Our third game was with Croatia. They were well organised but spent much of the match trying to engage us in a debate about the emergence of Eastern Europe as a fragmented, but forceful, power on the European stage. We won it fairly easily. Spooney did pretty well, but I credited both of his goals to myself.

By some weird twist of fate, the English national team followed an identical path to us. We'd both qualified for our respective quarter-finals, where we'd be playing Portugal. I'd heard that David Beckham wasn't having a great tournament and felt for the boy. If he wanted to experience real pressure, one day he should try being me.

For some reason the Portuguese saw themselves as the 'host' side and were getting more coverage on local TV than any of the other teams in the tournament. But I didn't let that intimidate me.

We were so pumped up before the match that we kicked off halfway through the national anthems. The Portuguese weren't particularly happy about this, especially as we scored, but they came back at us and equalised. At full time it was 2–2. We played the first half of extra time on tired shins and weary calves.

Unknown to me, as our match was going on a group of executives from UEFA (Pub Division) were watching us and the English national side on a split screen in one of those pretentious 'gastro' pubs that claim their food is cordon bleu, but is always scampi in a basket disguised as something else.

The executives had spent much of the evening marvelling at the disguises their portions of scampi in a basket were wearing. They agreed the Charlie Chaplin one was fantastic but Monica Lewinsky was unanimously voted the best.

They'd been arguing all evening about the whole notion of the 'penalty shoot-out'. They were sick and tired of games being decided in this crass and tasteless way. Realising that they couldn't completely get rid of penalties, they set out to devise some alterations that would make these events fairer and a far better spectacle for the crowds. As has been noted in the minutes of their meeting, their top five suggestions for adapting the traditional penalty shoot-out were:

- **All players have to wear stilts**

- **Penalties should be taken while blindfolded**
- **The ball must be hit with a garden rake**
- **An ugli fruit should be used instead of a ball**
- **The kicks should be taken while members of the opposing team tickle the taker**

Our match was running fifteen minutes behind the other England game. This was because the pub team game allowed a thirty-minute half time break for observers to purchase more alcohol.

So as we entered the second half of extra time, their game was ending in a 2–2 draw. As David Beckham walked forward to take the first penalty, the pub execs were still working on new penalty shoot-out ideas.

We all know now of course that the penalty spot in Beckham's game was a Portuguese-controlled molehill. If you look very carefully at the TV pictures, you'll see that as Beckham runs up to take the kick, an overfed mole sticks its head out and bites his Adidas Predator boot. This agonising nip forced Beckham to sky it well over the bar.

However, instead of feeling overcome with melancholy at this 'hoof', it was as if a light bulb (60 watts, long life) lit up in the execs' collective conscious.

'THAT'S IT!' they shouted deliriously, immediately contacting the referee in the pub game. My game.

'I'm in the middle of a match,' the ref declared angrily, 'can't you just text me?'

'NO!' came the reply.

So the ref halted the game and took the call. His eyes lit up when he heard what the execs were proposing. He was so distracted by this suggested initiative that when the call ended he spent a further couple of minutes trying in vain to make the camera on his phone work. He made a mental note to revisit the phone shop after the tournament. Who knows, they might even have a good pay-as-you-go offer on at the minute.

As our game slowed down and all twenty-two players took to crawling on all fours over the pitch, everyone knew that a draw was on the cards. And this meant penalties. After he'd blown at the end of extra time, the ref called both sets of players and managers together.

'Based on direct orders from UEFA (Pub Division),' he declared, 'tonight's penalty shoot-out will be won by the team that can *miss* the most goals.'

We were all astounded.

'You're joking?' asked Mr Vodaphone.

The ref slapped him across the face.

'That's for insolence under UEFA directive Z674C,' the ref explained.

With Mr Vodaphone running off to borrow an ice pack from our team of medics, I knew I needed to take the full captain's responsibility on my shoulders. I would be taking the first penalty.

As I walked up to the spot, I felt the nation's expectations accompanying my every stride. *Miss it* I willed myself.

I placed the ball carefully on the spot as their goalkeeper, Flickardo, tried to entice me with chicken from the barbecue he'd set up behind the goal.

'I'm a vegetarian,' I lied.

He quickly reached for a vegetable skewer, but I blanked him.

I ran up to the ball and slammed it as hard as I could, aiming for the corner flag. But to my utter devastation, an unexpected gust of wind pulled the ball into the goal.

Thankfully, the first Portuguese spot kicker also scored. Following that, every player on both sides successfully missed. When we'd all taken kicks, the ref indicated that anyone else connected with the teams could have a crack.

This meant that our kit people, medics, tea ladies and eventually fans were given the opportunity. As the two queues of kickers began to stretch for more than a mile out of town, the ref checked his watch. It was six seconds slow. He made a mental note to revisit the watch shop after the tournament. Who knows, they might even have a good offer on digital alarm clocks at the minute.

At 177 all it came round to my turn again.

The other lads whispered words of comfort at me as I headed back to the penalty spot.

'Don't fuck it up, Fecks' was one of them.

I searched for my wife and kids in the stands. It didn't take long to locate them. There was Vivian parading in some new leather coats on a specially designed catwalk in Block F. Chorlton-Cum-Hardy and King Lear were busy with their World's Most Reviled Dictators trump cards. It felt good that they were all so relaxed amidst the incredible tension.

To ensure I missed my kick, Mr Vodaphone quickly placed handcuffs on my wrists, chained me with leg irons and packed me inside a straitjacket. I toppled over several times as I approached the spot. Somehow, I managed to pull one of my legs back and made contact with the ball. It dribbled agonisingly towards the goal. Out of nowhere, a team of Portuguese curling players shimmied in front of the slowly moving ball, and brushed the grass in front of it. It reached the line. One of the Portuguese curlers shouted 'Look over there,' pointing to the other side of the stadium. We all looked, of course, and as we did so, he skilfully nudged the ball into the goal. It was the oldest trick in the book and, to a man, we fell for it.

It was now the Portuguese keeper's turn to take a kick. I willed him to score with every bone in my body, but he knew what he was doing. The ball rocketed out of the stadium and started heading for the Spanish border.

The Portuguese players went absolutely crazy. I thought their celebrations were a bit premature. For some reason my team mates sunk to the ground and lay face down on the turf like lifeless mannequins.

Mr Vodaphone looked gutted. His forehead seemed to have elongated a couple of centimetres during the evening.

'Cheer up gaffer,' I winked at him. He scowled back as another thirteen millimetres were added to his forehead.

The plane journey home was very quiet. At the request of the rest of the team, I travelled in the hold. It was so decent of them – I could stretch out on the softer pieces of luggage and sleep.

And now I sit here on a warm Spanish evening. The fig tree in my apartment's bathroom is doing well, and I can now order pie and mash in Spanish.

I'm constantly hearing rumours about my future. Uncle Terry phoned me recently and said loads of people with clubs were after me. I asked him to name some of them, but he just told me to keep a low profile and hung up.

Earlier today I was feeling a bit restless so I walked the dog. It wasn't my dog, it was one I found tied to some railings, but it looked like it needed some exercise. Within minutes, I found myself in one of the city's elegant shopping malls, where I bought a bottle of Coke for me and some beef jerky for the dog, and sat down on a wall.

I felt a tap on my shoulder. I turned round and there, in the flesh, was David Beckham. He was sitting next to me, also holding a Coke bottle.

'Becks,' I said with surprise and delight.

'Fecks,' he grinned.

A whole scrapbook of photos flashed through my mind.

'Do you remember when we first met each other?' I said, 'we agreed that whoever made it to the England team first, would have a Coke bought for them by the other one.'

'Course I do,' he replied wistfully. 'I like Fanta more now, but the principle remains.'

'Well I suppose we both got there at about the same time,' I said.

'Yeah,' he agreed thoughtfully.

I instinctively lifted up my Coke bottle and handed it over to him. He wrapped his fingers around it gratefully. Sensing the significance of the moment, he was about to walk off with both bottles, but my coughing fit alerted him as to the appropriate response. He slowly handed me his bottle.

'Cheers,' he said.

'Cheers,' I replied.

'Cheers,' said the dog, straining at his leash and overheating under the mall's glaring lights.

Becks and I unscrewed the bottle caps and drank heartily.

He downed his in one gulp and jumped off the wall. He offered me his hand. I offered him mine. We shook.

'I'll still follow your progress,' he grinned.

'I'll follow yours, too,' I replied, 'even though sometimes it's hard to find out anything about what you're up to.'

With that he strolled off to his bodyguards, who ushered him into his executive people carrier. He turned back and gave me a quick wave.

And then he was gone.

I polished off my Coke and gave the frothy bit at the bottom to the dog.

As I started walking back home, I thought about the future. There was so much to look forward to. Sure, there'll be ups and downs in football as in life, but I wouldn't have it any other way. I smiled to myself. I knew I could handle whatever it was that awaited me.

Bring it on, I whispered softly to myself.

And then, at the top of my voice, scaring a party of pensioners from Morecambe, *BRING IT ON!!!!!!!*

CAREER RECORD

Full name: David David Feckham (like Boutros Boutros-Ghali's parents, mine also gave me the same middle and first names)
Place and Date of Birth: Leytonstone, April 1st 1975
Parents: Sheila and Reg or Reg and Sheila
Sisters: Katie (with a K) and Clare (with a C)
Married: Can't find copy of *Weddings That Went Horribly Wrong*, but when I do will be able to add date in here
Wife: Vivian Lucy Lisa Des'ree Juliette Gaye Norma Howard Gerald Bette Anna Lucy Lisa Nicola Fox
Sons: Chorlton-Cum-Hardy Didsbury Feckham b. 1999, King Lear Feckham b. 2002
Height: 5ft 180cm (11 inches)
Weight: 11st 75kg (13lb)

Early Career

Kickabouts with Dad in front room – 401
Goals: Dad 5,792 Me 6
Own Goals: Dad 0 Me 401
Record: W0 D0 L401
Honours: None

Kickabouts with Dad in park – 891
Goals: Dad 47,012 Me 0
Own Goals: Dad 0 Me 891
Record: W0 D0 L891
Honours: None

Kickabouts in my own room in middle of night – 1,936
Goals: Me 15,807 Dad (caught me at it one night and joined in) 48
Own Goals: Dad 0 Me 1,936
Record: W1,935 D0 L1
Honours: Best player ever to have a kickabout in my own room in the middle of the night 1980, '81, '82, '83, '84, '85

Games at the Dump – 45
Goals: 0
Own Goals: 45
Record: W0 D0 L45
Honours: None

Games on grass pitch behind paper factory – 104
Goals: 0
Own goals: 104
Record: W0 D0 L104
Honours: None

Games outside really quiet sub post offices in village near Southend – 1
Goals: Me 1 (pen)
Own goals: Me 0
Record: W1 D0 L0 (100% record)
Honours: 2p

Games for Bridgeway Novas – 35
Goals: 1
Own Goals: 35
Record: W0 D1 L34
Honours: 1 league title

Schnitzel and Parrot

Junior team: (North West Sector 7 Junior Pub League)
Games: 26
Goals: 0
Own goals: 102
Record: W0 D0 L26
Honours: None

Senior team: (South by South East Manchester Pub
Sunday League Division 4 (North))
Games: 190
Goals: 0
Own goals: 190
Record: W1 D0 L189
Honours: None

Fun in the Sun Timeshare Apartments Ltd XI (West Costa Del Sol League Division 6 (South))

Games (So far): 15
Goals (So far): 0
Own goals (So far) 15
Record (So far): W0 (So far) D0 (So far) L15 (So far)
Honours (So far): None

England Pub Sunday League Side

Pub Sunday League World Cup (France '98)
Games: 1
Goals: 0
Own goals: 0
Record: W0 D0 L1
Sent off: 1

Pub Sunday League World Cup (Japansouthkorea '02 qualifying and tournament)
Games: 7
Goals: 0
Own goals: 7
Record: W4 D2 L1

Pub Euro 2004 (Portugal 2004)

Games: 4
Goals: 2 (pens, should have missed, could count as own goals)
Own Goals: 2 (pens, should have missed, do count as own goals)
Record: W2 D0 L2

OVERALL RECORD (including kickabouts in front room, park and bedroom)

Games: 3,656
Goals: 15,817
Own goals: 3,728
Record: W1,931 D3 L1,710

OVERALL RECORD (excluding kickabouts in front room, park and bedroom)

Games: 428
Goals: 4
Own goals: 500
Record: W8 D3 L415

INDEX